THE FANG

CHRONICLES OF THE SKY RUNNERS

SCOTT ALEXANDER WILLIAMS

Parchment Global Publishing
1500 Market Street, 12th Floor, East Tower
Philadelphia, Pennsylvania, 19102
www.parchmentglobalpublishing.com

ISBN: 978-1-952302-13-8 (hc)
ISBN: 978-1-952302-11-4 (sc)
ISBN: 978-1-952302-12-1 (e)

CONTENTS

NEW ORDERS

Rebecca Van Stocks was walking to the door to one of the conference rooms of the Vatican. As she got closer she could hear two people yelling at each other. When she got to the door she opened it a little, and the creaking of the door made the two men turn. The slight opening was enough for Cardinal Staff, the Vatican's head of military operations and Matthew Duncan, the head Intelligence officer for the Vatican, to see Rebecca. She stepped in a little farther and Cardinal Staff said, "Rebecca. . . Come on in, it is nice to see you up and about now."

She had been recovering from the last battle at the island of Crete. For all intents and purposes, it was a disaster. The vampire group called the Fang; had gotten themselves a dirty nuclear bomb and are planning on using it to destroy the Vatican. Everything went wrong the moment they hit the base, Rebecca almost didn't make it out of there and her assistant didn't. Mike was shot down just outside the camp at the landing site. Rebecca kept her focus on Cardinal Staff; he was a father-like figure. He stood about six-foot-tall, had gray hair, and wore the normal Cardinal outfit. She smiled at him.

"Thank you, Cardinal, but I don't want to interrupt you two. I will come back again in a few minutes."

"Non-sense, besides you are the topic of our discussion."

"I was afraid you would say that."

"We are thinking..."

"We are thinking about bringing Gabriel back in." Matthew interrupted the Cardinal. Matthew was a little taller than Cardinal, he stood about six foot two and had black hair. He was a little tanned, seemed to always wear a black suit with solid colored ties and had only been at the job as Intel officer for about a year now. Rebecca gave him a disapproving look.

"I don't think we need to go and bring him back. Besides, wandering around the United States looking for Gabriel would be a waste of time. He has been gone for over two hundred years now and if he was to come back, I would think that he would have done that by now."

"Well, it seems that we need him. After the last battle, it looks like we need the help."

"What we need is better intelligence, Matthew." Rebecca felt a little offended by the comment, "We were not prepared for that battle. And who is the Intel officer, oh, yeah, that is you Matt."

"I gave you all that we had, you needed to adjust.

"Look you two," Cardinal interrupted, "I agree with you Rebecca, we needed better Intelligence but Matt may be right. I think we should go and see if we can bring him back."

Rebecca walked up to whisper in the Cardinal's ear, "Cardinal, don't you think that I can handle it?"

"I do, but there is more going on here than what we are seeing. Gabe can get to the bottom of all of this."

"But Cardinal, I can do this. We don't need him; let me have another shot at them. I will get that bomb."

"Rebecca, I have no doubt that you can get the bomb. I want Gabe in for other reasons." Rebecca put her head down, she felt that she lost the trust that they had built up. Cardinal lifted her head, "Look, you are one of the best that we have had since Gabriel has left, but we need to get him in to find out what is going on. Once he is done with this mission, he can go home and we will leave him alone. Does that sound like a plan?"

"Do you think that he can get to the bottom of all of this?"

"Yes I do."

"Okay…"

Matthew was feeling left out, "If you want me to get the right people together, I think you need to include me in on the conversation."

Rebecca looked at him as if to say, why are you interrupting us, "Okay, we will bring him back in, since we can't get the good Intel that we need. On one condition, that once we have the bomb, he can go back if he wants to."

"Good, we could use the experience that he will bring. I will find someone to go and get him."

"No Matt, I will do that," Cardinal informed him. "Come, Rebecca, we will go to the Hall of Records and find the last address we have for him." He grabbed Rebecca's arm and led her out of the conference room.

As they were walking across Saint Peter's Square, Cardinal quietly said to Rebecca, "I want you to go and get Gabriel."

Rebecca stopped in the middle of the Square. Cardinal took a couple of steps farther and then turned around to look at Rebecca. She had a shocked look on her face; "Shouldn't I stay here and help with the defenses of the Vatican? One of the troops can handle going to get Gabriel."

Cardinal took a step closer to her, as not to let unwanted ears to hear him,

"I think that this needs a personal touch. You have been doing his job for the last eighty years. If I send someone that has not been at this as long and is not doing his job, he may just write them off and not come back at all. Plus you have been in many battles that were once his. He will be able to relate to you and you to him."

"But Cardinal--."

Cardinal held out his hand, "Do this for me, if anything else, do it for me. You are not only one of my commanders you are my friend and so I am asking this as a friend."

"How can I say no to that?"

"Your right, you can't. That is why I said it."

She gave him a smile, "Okay, I will go, for you." She started to walk again and put her arm around Cardinal's arm.

When they got to the Hall of Records, Cardinal went up to the front desk, "Excuse me Jane; I need to get into the Secured Section Gamma."

"Do you have your access card Cardinal?"

"Yes, I do." Cardinal opened his wallet up and pulled out the access card. He handed it to Jane, "Anything else?"

"Yes, put your finger on the panel to get your identity verified."

He placed his finger on the panel and when a light next to the panel showed green he lifted it again. Jane smiled at him,

"Okay, you will need to slide your card again at the door and then put in your access code. Will that be all?"

"Yes, I need to sign in Rebecca Van Stocks."

After Rebecca was signed in they went to the section to get the information that they needed. It took them about an hour, going through paperwork after paperwork. Finally, Rebecca spoke up, "Is this it?"

Cardinal walked over to her, looked at the paper, "Yep, that is it."

"Where in the world is Williamsville, Nebraska?"

"You are about to find out, Rebecca."

CHAPTER 2

THE FANG

The dark warehouse was suddenly brightened up when the roof opened up and sunlight shined in. A helicopter hovered over the opening and when the roof stopped opening, the helicopter landed in the middle of the warehouse. The helicopter was white and the windows were blocked out by a metal plate that slid in front of them from the inside. As the engines shut off, the sky doors to the warehouse closed. Once the warehouse was dark again, men came out from one of the side doors. Lights then came on and started to light up the place. One of the men went up to the helicopter and opened the passenger door. A female stepped out; she was about five foot five inches tall. She had a black skin-tight jumpsuit on and a hooded cape. Her ears were pointed; her skin was pale, eyes yellow, long black hair and looked about twenty-five years of age. Another male came up to her, "Melina madam, I am glad to see you. Welcome to the new headquarters."

"Spare me the pleasantries, Steve. I am not happy that we had to move our operations here in the first place. Just give me the update on the bomb."

"Yes madam, the scientist thinks that the detonator will be done by the end of this week, but we are still having a problem hiding the bomb's radiation."

"Tell them if we don't hide that radiation, then we might as well not do the mission. If that happens, then I will call it a failure and they don't want me to call it that."

"Well... um... Madam, they do have an idea. They know of a scientist in Berlin that might be able to hide the radiation."

"Well then what are you waiting for, go get him and bring him here. You know the drill by now. For crying out loud your father was a founding member."

"The founding member madam and I was just waiting for the orders."

"I keep on forgetting, you don't work like the United States military, and they don't need orders to do their jobs. Now, leave and I don't want to see you until you have the Doctor in your hands."

"Yes madam..."

Steve bowed and walked away. Melina continued to the door where the men came out of. When she got there a female approached,

"Melina madam, someone is on the phone for you."

"Thank you Jessica, I will take it in my office."

She began to walk away, but then turned around,

"Ah, Jessica... I just got here so where is my office?"

Jessica smiled at her, "Follow me."

Once in her office, the light on the phone was blinking indicating that someone was on hold. Melina picked up the receiver and cleared her throat before saying, "This is Melina?"

A deep male voice came over the phone, "Melina... I just got word that the Vatican is going to send someone to get Gabriel."

"Gabriel; the Gabriel? Who is going to get him?"

"No word on that, but if I would guess the Cardinal, he would send Rebecca."

"When is she leaving?"

"I am going to guess tonight. I know you have never met Gabe, but he is not one to mess with."

"I remember stories about him many years ago, but what do you think we should do about this?"

"The only thing possible, get that bomb ready now. So the next question is, what is the status of the bomb?"

"The detonator is almost done. It should be done by the end of this month."

"You said that it would be done by the end of last month, why is it taking so long?"

"We had to leave the island of Crete after the attack, and we are having--."

"No more excuses Melina, I want that thing done by the end of this month or I will find someone else to do the job."

Melina knew what that meant. People just don't get fired around here. If you lose your job, you lose more than that. Melina straightened herself, "You won't need to do that sir, but give me a little bit of time. We are having problems hiding the radiation. We do have a solution though and it is getting worked on right now."

"Very well, I will give you until the middle of the next month, but it better be done then."

"Yes sir, we are sending --."

"I don't care about the details Melina, you know that, just get it done."

"Yes sir, it will be done."

At that, the man hung up and Melina put the phone down. She walked out to see Jessica at her desk, "I am going to get some rest and you need to do the same. I know you have been up all morning getting the office ready. Have one of the day workers watch the desk and go and get some rest."

"Yes madam, do you want me to show you where your room is?"

"Yes, that would be nice."

Jessica put her things down on the desk and walked with Melina to the tunnels.

CHAPTER 3

LEAVING ROME

Cardinal had been in the car waiting for Rebecca for some time now. They had stopped at a warehouse not too far from the Vatican. She told him that she wanted to pick something up. Finally, he saw her walking out, but something was different. Her outfit, that only appeared when evil was nearby, was out.

"What is going on? Is there a problem?"

"No problem Cardinal."

"Then why is your outfit visible?"

"Because of this..." Rebecca pulled out a pendant that was attached to a chain around her neck and hidden under her shirt. It was covered in plastic to keep it from touching her clothes. Cardinal Staff looked at it,

"Why do you have that?"

"Because, I don't think Gabriel is going to show himself to me, so I'm bringing this along. It will force his clothes to change and bring out his outfit."

"Good idea Rebecca. Did you want to go to your apartment before we head to the airport?"

"Of course, I need to pick up some other clothes and I need my hygiene kit for the trip."

They drove to the apartment close to the Vatican. The apartment that Rebecca lived in was the same apartment that Gabriel had before

10

he left. After packing some stuff and putting her bags by the door, she went into her bedroom and wrote down in her diary.

Back downstairs Cardinal Staff helped Rebecca with her bags. On the way to the airport, Cardinal asked, "How long do you think this will take?"

"I don't think it will take me too long. The longest part is going to be finding him. All we have is the name of the town; we don't have an address for him. But if I were to make a guess at it, I would say about Friday or Saturday we should be back here and getting ready to go."

"Since today is Sunday, you think this will take about a week to do this?"

"There about.

"You know you won't get to Omaha until Monday morning, right?"

"Cardinal... I think that once Gabriel finds out what kind of danger the Vatican is in, he will come back as fast as possible."

"Well, I hope you are right. You will have the Vatican 747 as long as you need it, but we will need you back here by Friday of next week so we can plan before they deploy that bomb. You have until then."

"Sounds good, but I don't think I'll need that time. Make sure that the General knows what to expect, and make sure he has all corners of Rome covered, and, ah, make sure..."

"Rebecca, the General knows what to do."

"I know, I'm just nervous about the safety of the Vatican."

"Is it the safety of the Vatican or is it something else, or someone else?"

"Maybe a little bit of both. I mean, he's a legend in his own right."

"You'll do just fine. You can't be having second thoughts already?"

"Cardinal, what if I can't convince him? I don't what to be pushy at the same time."

"Like you said, once he finds out the danger that the Vatican is in, he'll come straight away."

"But he has stayed away for such a long time. I fear that if I push him too much, it will just confirm the whole reason he left in the first place."

"Take a deep breath." Cardinal waited until she was done taking a breath, "You are the reason I'm sending you. Use your connection that you have to him. I believe in you."

"Cardinal, thank you."

The Cardinal smiled at her. At the airport, Cardinal Staff pulled up to the Vatican 747. The two got out while one of the flight attendants went and grabbed Rebecca's bags out of the car. Rebecca and Cardinal Staff walked up to the steps to the plane. After Rebecca took a couple of steps up she noticed that Cardinal Staff was not following her, she turned to him,

"Are you not coming with me? I mean you are from the United States, this is your home."

"I'm from Denver, Colorado; the United States is not like the countries here in Europe, where when you enter the country you are home. The United States is a lot bigger and besides, I want you to do this one alone. The two of us might throw Gabriel off and I do need to stay here and make sure Matthew doesn't explode and destroy the Vatican himself when he finds out that I sent you to get Gabriel. Consider this a vacation, so try to enjoy yourself while you are there."

"Okay, I will see you when I get back then."

"I will see both of you, when you get back here."

Rebecca smiled, gave Cardinal Staff a hug and then went up the steps to the door of the plane. Cardinal Staff stood at the bottom and watch Rebecca as she got to the top. By the door the Captain was waiting for her and he informed her, "We are ready to go when you are madam."

Rebecca turned to look at Cardinal, waved and then went in the plane. Cardinal waved back and said to himself under his breath, "Good luck and God Bless."

The Captain walked in, closed the door and the steps were pushed away. Inside, Rebecca was walking past the command center and conference room. Found her seat next to the window. There were a few of her troops in the plane talking among themselves. Rebecca paid no attention to them, put her seat belt on and pulled out a piece of paper that she had folded in her pocket as the plane started to taxi to the runway. Rebecca looked down at the paper that had the direction to Williamsville, Nebraska, and she thought to herself, *Where in the world is Williamsville, Nebraska and why would Gabriel move there?* She turned her focus out the window as the plane was taking off, thinking… *Well, as Cardinal said, I'm about to find out.*

CHAPTER 4

GABRIEL

The sun was shining brightly over the fields. The only sound that Gabriel could hear was the sound of the John Deere tractor. Gabriel had been working in the fields for most of the day. Fieldwork was not only quiet, which Gabriel liked, but at times it can be relaxing. Gabriel was about five foot nine inches tall, he had brown hair, brown eyes, was slender, lightly tanned from farming day in, day out and he always wore leather gloves to hide the crosses scarred in his palms. His thoughts would sometimes go to the many battles that he had been in and sometimes they would go to his family that he lost over two thousand years ago. Then they would go back to the fighting evil that he did following the death of his family. The many battles that he had while fighting for the Vatican. When he left the Vatican over two hundred years ago, he did not tell anyone where he was going and moved to the Americas. Gabriel got to the East end of the field, turned the tractor to go down the other way and saw a pickup truck on the road in front of this field. He started to head West on the field. As he got closer, he could see a man get out of the pickup truck. It was a white Ford F-150 that Gabriel recognized as belonging to Tom the grain elevator operator. Tom walked down from the road and onto the field as Gabriel got close. Tom was about five foot ten inches tall; he wore blue jeans and a tan button-up shirt. His hair was brown and was a slender man. He was thirty-nine years old but didn't look it. When

Gabriel reached the end of the field he stopped the tractor and got out. As he walked up to Tom he gave him a smile,

"So Tom, did you come out here to see your income grow?"

Returning the smile, "No... I came out to see if you were still alive."

"What do you mean?"

"Well, I have been trying to get a hold of you all day. What, are you going around with your cell phone off now?"

"No... I don't have my cell phone with me. I didn't want to have people calling me."

"Why? Isn't that the whole reason for having a cell phone, so that people can get ahold of you?"

"Yes, but that becomes a problem when you want some peace and quiet."

"Well, you do have a point there.

"So you came all the way out here for a reason, what did you want?"

"Oh... I want to tell you that the speculators are going to be doing their estimates next week and you know that it doesn't, if never, go in the farm's favor. So did you want to sell some corn before they make the predictions?"

"What do I have in town right now?"

"Come with me to the pickup and I will look it up."

The two walked back up to the road where the pickup was. Tom reached in and grabbed his laptop, pulled it out of the cab of the pickup and then went to the tailgate, put it down and put the computer on it so that Gabriel could see what he was doing. He opened it up and pushed a couple of buttons. The computer came to life and Tom went and opened a file on the desktop. After scrolling down a little he informed Gabriel,

"It looks like you have about five hundred bushels of corn in town right now. Did you want to sell?"

"What are the prices of corn right now?"

"It's at three dollars and eighty-five cents."

"Yah... Let's go ahead and sell all of it."

"Great, did you want to bring in anymore?"

"No, I will hold off until later."

"Okay, I will be putting one thousand nine hundred twenty-five dollars in your account. Did you want it in your Williamsville account?"

"Yes if you could please."

"Very well... I will need you to come in and sign the receipt."

"Okay, I will be in tomorrow."

Tom closed his laptop, walked around and put the computer back into the cab of the pickup. Then Tom just remembered something that happened earlier that day.

"Oh... By the way Gabe. Do you know someone named Rebecca umm, Stocks I think it was?"

"No... I don't recall that name. Why do you ask?"

"Well because she was in town looking for you today.

"Looking for me? What did she look like?"

"Well let me see here, she was about five six; five seven, reddish hair, she had a blue top on and black pants. But that wasn't the strangest part."

"What was the strangest part?"

"She was wearing these colors in the month of June."

"What is so strange about that? Many young kids do that today. How old was she, do you think?"

"I would say about twenty to twenty-five, but did I tell you that she was wearing a trench coat?"

"No... You didn't tell me that, now that is strange." At that, Gabe thought about his trench coat that comes out when evil is nearby. Heat doesn't affect him even with the trench coat on. *But then again, would it had been possible for someone with the same blessing to have their outfit out here in Williamsville?* Gabe thought to himself. That was the reason he came out here, very little evil to deal with.

"And you said that she was looking for me?"

"Yep... I was at the bar having something to eat at noon today and she came walking in looking for you or if anyone knows where she could find you."

"Did anyone tell her where I am?"

"No, I don't think so."

"Well, maybe I will come across her tomorrow when I come in to sign my receipt."

"I hope so, she seemed like a very nice young female and since you're alone and always seem to wear those black gloves she might be right up your ally."

"You are not trying to play matchmaker are you, Tom?"

"No... Of course not." Tom smiled at Gabe and then looked down at his watch and saw what time it was.

"Wow, it is three-thirty already. I need to get back into town. I will talk to you tomorrow then."

"Yah... Talk to you later."

Tom got back into his pickup and drove off. Gabe went back down into his fields and finished the field that he was working on, but the whole time the thought of this person looking for him was on his mind.

Later on that evening, Gabe was sitting in his living room. The television was on but Gabe was not paying any attention to it. He looked at the time, it was about seven thirty and Gabe went to get something to eat. He got up and drove into town. Williamsville was only four miles away and it was a small town, the town had only four hundred fifty people. Gabe liked it because of its size; evil didn't go around there too much. As Gabe drove through the town, he went in front of Saint Peter's Catholic Church. He looked into the parking lot and saw a black Buick that he had not seen before. Being such a small town, he knew almost every car that the people owned, but this one was not one for the town's people. It was sitting by Father Scott's car. The person that Tom was talking about came to mind on which the car might belong to. Gabe pulled in to get a better look at the car. He parked right behind the car and then got out, walked up to the car and looked into the window. At about that time Father Scott came walking out of the Rectory. He saw Gabe looking into the car and walked up to him.

"Gabe... It is nice to see you."

Gabe looked up from looking into the car, "Why is that?"

"Well there is a nice young female here looking for you. Rebecca Van Stocks I think her name is."

"Well, where is she?"

"She is in Saint Ann's Chapel in the back of the church."

"Really???"

"Yes, I was about to give her your address, but since you are here, you can talk to her now."

At that, they heard the door to the back chapel open up and saw a woman walk out. A glow was starting to show around Gabe and he could feel his swords start to appear behind him. Shocked, Gabe went back to his car as fast as possible. The only time Gabe's outfit comes out without him willing it, is when evil is nearby. Since he didn't bring them out himself that only could mean that evil was nearby and it only happened when this woman came out of the chapel. Gabe got into the car and drove off. Father Scott was shocked to see Gabe leave so fast and see the glow around Gabe. The woman ran up to Father Scott and asked,

"Who was that Father?"

"That was Gabriel, but I don't..."

"Do you have his address?!" She said with excitement.

"Ah... Yes... Here..." Father handed the piece of paper to her and she took off as fast as Gabe did.

Gabe was hoping that by leaving, the woman would follow him to his home and leave Father Scott out of the way of any fight that might come about. This way she couldn't use Father as a human shield. When he got back to his house he ran in and pulled off his gloves. His clothes went back to normal when he left the town, but now was a waiting game to see if she took the bait. He didn't have to wait too long. A bright glow began to show around him and his clothes changed. His swords came out and he walk out the door to see the black Buick pulling into his driveway. Gabe thought to himself, *She is here, here we go...*

C H A P T E R   5

THE PACKAGE

"Melina madam.

"Yes, Jessica?" Melina had just gotten up and was going to her office when Jessica saw her,

"I just got word from Steve that he has the package in hand and is on his way back right now."

"Very good. Did he say if he had all the packages?"

"Yes, he does."

"Good, when he gets here have him put the package in the south warehouse."

"Yes, madam…"

Melina walked into her office and sat down at the desk. She tried to start the computer up but it was not comm. g on. Melina hit the button on her desk and Jessica's voice came over the speaker.

"Yes, madam?"

"Why is my computer not working?"

"We don't have all the power systems up and running. I will make sure that they get you running as fast as possible."

"Very well… Let me know when they are done."

"Yes, madam…"

Melina released the button and sat back in her chair. She hated not having anything to do and waiting for things to get done. After a minute or so she decided to get up and walk around to get herself familiar with the new camp. Malina stepped out of her office, "Jessica,

19

I am going for a walk; let me know when they are done with my computer."

"Yes, madam... "Jessica promptly responded.

Since it was night time Melina walked from one warehouse to another. When she entered the warehouse with her helicopter, Jim her pilot walked up to her,

"Melina madam. . . I was wondering? I can get together a group of soldiers and go to the United States and attack Gabriel to keep him from wanting to come back."

"No... We don't want to do that."

"But madam…"

"Look, we don't even know where he is and you will have to be looking all over the country for him, plus, if we attack him at his home town he may feel that he has to come back just to protect the town. Good that you want to take the fight to him, but I think it will backfire on us in the end."

"Very well madam. If you need anything, I will be in my office over there." Jim pointed to an office in the corner of the warehouse.

Melina nodded and continued to look around the camp.

CHAPTER 6

ENCOUNTER

Rebecca was walking out of the back chapel of Saint Peter's Catholic Church when she spotted Father Scott talking to a man. Suddenly a bright glow showed around him and Rebecca knew that it must be Gabriel. He took off back to a tan Chevy Cavalier and drove off very fast. Rebecca walked up to Father Scott and asked,

"Who was that Father?"

"That was Gabriel, but I don't..."

"Do you have his address?!" She said with excitement.

"Ah. . . Yes. . . Here..." Father handed the piece of paper to her and she took off as fast as possible after Gabriel. Father just stood there and watched Rebecca drive away very fast. He had a shocked look on his face. Rebecca was racing down the highway and when she went over a bridge that covered a creek she could see the Cavalier going down a gravel road and disappear behind a group of trees. The sun was setting and she didn't want to miss the opportunity to talk to Gabriel. So she kept her focus on the spot that she last saw Gabriel's car and drove to that place. As she approached the trees she could see a driveway and a mailbox on the other side of the trees. He had to have driven in there, she thought to herself. She pulled into the yard and then, by the garage was the tan Cavalier. She stopped the car in front of the house by the field up ahead. As she got out she could see Gabriel coming out of his house and his outfit out, what looked like a black cassock, black pants black trench coat, black hat and swords at the ready. Gabriel took a good look at her and saw that she had two katana swords sticking out from behind her trench coat. Gabriel spoke up first,

"Who are you?"

"I'm Rebecca Van Stocks, the Vatican has sent me." Rebecca responded,

"The Vatican, forgive me but I don't believe you. You see, I can sense evil and this outfit only comes out when evil is nearby. You are the only one here and my senses are pointing to you."

"But I was on holy ground."

"Yes, I am still wondering about that. But you may be a new product of Backular."

"Look Gabriel, the evil that you are sensing is the pendant that I have around my neck." At that Rebecca pulled out the pendant from her shirt and lifted it over her head. She held it out in front of Gabriel so that he could see that it was the pendant and not Rebecca that he was sensing. Gabriel looked at that pendant and said,

"Prove it, throw it away somewhere, then come back and stand in front of me so that I can get a good sense of you." Secretly Gabriel can see evil, it showed up as red, but the pendant blocked what he could sense from Rebecca.

Rebecca looked around and then walked to the road, continued to the other side and threw the pendant into the field. She then walked back to her car to show that she was not evil. As she was walking back, a bright glow showed around her and Gabriel as their clothes changed back to normal. When Gabriel saw Rebecca's clothes, he knew that she had gotten the same blessing that he had gotten almost two thousand years ago. When she was in front of her car again Gabriel said, "Okay, come on in."

Rebecca smiled and followed Gabriel in to the house. He directed her to the kitchen. There was a long table on one side of the kitchen, Gabriel then said, "Please, have a seat." And pointed to one of the chairs at the table.

As she took a seat she introduced herself, "Like I said before, I'm Rebecca Van Stocks. I have been doing the job that you had at the Vatican for the last eighty years."

"Nice to meet you, Rebecca. Do you want something to drink?"

"Well if you have tea that would be nice." Rebecca smiled at the hospitality, but by the tone of his voice, she could tell that he also wasn't pleased to see someone from the Vatican at his home either.

"I have ice tea, is that okay?"

"That will be fine."

Gabriel went to the fridge, pulled out a pitcher of tea and then went to the covert and pulled out two glasses.

He walked to the table, poured the tea in one glass, and handed it to Rebecca, "Did you want sugar?"

"No, I'm fine."

After he poured his own he sat down at the other end of the table. Rebecca then spoke up, "I am glad to see that you have not lost your hospitality."

"Well, I do get guest every so often. So let's get down to business. Why did the Vatican send you?"

"We need your help, Gabriel."

"Gabe... just call me Gabe."

"Okay, Gabe. . . We have a problem that we need your help with."

"Well, it looks to me that they have their help right in front of me."

"I am not as equipped to be handling this kind of threat."

"What is the threat?"

"The Fang... You should remember them." Gabe nodded to confirm that he remembered them. "Well they have gotten themselves a dirty nuclear bomb and they are planning to use it to blow up the Vatican." Rebecca thought that at that point Gabe would just, jump up and get ready to go, but to her surprise he said, "Then why are you here to find me. You should be back in Rome trying to find them and destroy that bomb, or do you have others with the same blessing?"

"No, I'm the only one with the blessing. But I am here because we had already tried to stop them once."

"And you failed?"

"Sadly, yes."

"But we are talking about the Fang. They don't do anything in a large group, they always fight in small groups and all you have to do is find the group that has the bomb and destroy that group."

"And a year ago I would have agreed with you, but now they are fighting as one group."

"It took you off guard, didn't it?"

"Yes, we almost didn't make it out of there."

Gabe put his elbows on the table, put his hands up and dropped his face into his hands. Then looked back up at Rebecca, "Then why don't you just adjust your attack and get that bomb."

"Look Gabe, I had the same idea, but they insisted that I come here to get you, now are you coming back with me or not?" Rebecca wanted an answer now and was getting tired of the questions.

"Well, like I said, they have their man, or rather, their woman right here and you need to be there to plan the next attack and soon."

"So that is a no?"

"Rebecca, I was doing that job for over two thousand years. I am done with it. They got you now and I am sure that you can handle whatever comes up."

"So you are just going to turn your back on the Church you swore to protect?"

"Rebecca..."

Rebecca held out her hand to stop him, "Look... You don't have to decide tonight. I am going to be here until Friday of next week. You have until then to make up your mind. Is that a deal?"

Gabe took a deep breath and let it out, looked up Rebecca, gave her a small smile, "I doubt you are going to change my mind on this one, but you are free to stay here as long as you think." Gabe looked at the clock and noticed that it was almost nine o'clock. He looked at Rebecca, "Look... It is getting late, do you have a place to stay at yet?"

Rebecca smiled, "No... I was just going to get a place in that 'BIGGER' town across the river." She was poking fun at the size of town that Gabe had moved to.

Gabe returned the smile, "Well, I do have a spare bedroom here, if you don't mind fighting the bugs for the bed?" He likes the idea of loosening up the air.

"I guess I can handle it. Besides, I will be able to talk to you when I need to then."

"Then...it is a plan, let's go get your bags out of the car."

The two went outside and Rebecca opened the trunk of the car. Gabe looked in and saw three bags. One big one and two small ones. Being the gentleman that Gabe is, he grabbed the big one. When he felt how heavy it was he asked, "What? Did you pack the kitchen sink?"

"No... Not this time, this time I packed the washroom sink. I need to do some laundry while I am here."

"You know we have a great new invention called a washer and dryer, don't you?"

"Really? You have the technology here in Nebraska. I was told that you are still behind in that sort of stuff."

"Surprise, surprise. . . Welcome to the twenty-first century."

Gabe carried the bag in and took them downstairs where the spear bedroom was. He showed Rebecca the bathroom that she can use and when he was sure that she was settled in he went back upstairs to get ready to go to bed.

CHAPTER 7

THE DOCTOR

Doctor Kosch was tied down to a chair in this dark room. He could tell that it was a warehouse by the echoing of the room, but most of the warehouse was pitch black. The only light that was shining was the light on him and it kept blinding him whenever he tried to look around. There were four people standing close by and his family was not too far away. He could hear them every so often. A few hours ago he was sitting at home with his family and then several men broke in, grabbed him and his family and put hoods over them. All at once everything went black when he tried to protest by pushing back on one of the men. When he woke, his head hurt, he was tied down in this warehouse and no one would say anything. He kept yelling out,

"Someone, speak to me! Why are you holding us?" But the men around him didn't say a word, "Please say something!"

Finally after an hour of protesting, trying to get an answer he heard a female voice say,

"They will not answer you, doctor."

It was not any of his family so Doctor Kosch asked, "Who is there? Why are you holding us?"

A slender female came out of the darkness and into the middle of the light in front of him. She was wearing a black skin-tight jumpsuit and a hooded cape. Her hair was black and looked very pale,

"I'm Melina doc. I am in need of your assistance."

He took a good look at her, "If you need a doctor, you got the wrong person. I am not that kind of doctor. I'm a nuclear physicist."

Melina smiled; she knew that he was referring to her pale looking skin. She spoke up again, "That, my doctor, is what we are looking for."

"Why are you looking for a nuclear physicist?"

"Well, you see doctor. We have this little problem. We found an old nuclear device here on this island and the only way to get rid of it is to fly it out of here on a helicopter or by boat. So we are putting it in a suitcase, but we are having a problem reducing the radiation."

"And you need me to help you out on that?"

"Yes, otherwise we will get sick and we don't want anyone else to get sick from this."

"Why didn't you just call me and ask, I would have come here as fast as possible to save lives?"

"I am sorry, but Steve was afraid that you would have said no."

"Okay, why then tie me up and hold my family as well?"

"Again, I am sorry about that." Melina snapped her fingers and the men around the doctor untied him. As the last of the ropes were untied Doctor Kosch asked,

"I know that I am not going to like the answer, but what if I said no?"

Melina leaned over the chair, putting her hands on the armrests to give the doctor a good look at her and said, "Then I will kill your family one by one." At that point he could see her ears were pointed. She let her fangs grow out and her eyes turned yellow as she smiled at him. It shocked the doctor so much that he jumped backward in his chair. Melina stood straight,

"Get him to work on the case right away."

One of them responded, "Yes madam…"

They reached down and carried him to the location of the case and a glass lab for him to work in.

CHAPTER 8

THE NEXT DAY

Jerusalem A.D. 52

Gabe was walking with Paul to this man's house that he just met. He had been with Paul for weeks now, learning about this man named Jesus Christ. Now this other man named Peter was to give him a new blessing. A blessing that God had promised him in a dream. Before the dream, Gabe believed in many gods and now he was being told that there is only one God and Jesus is his son. That took Gabe by surprise at first. When he started his mission centuries ago to destroy evil, God told him that he was to do it until the second coming of his son and since he believed in the gods of the Greeks he thought that Hercules was a son of the god Zeus, but now he knows that there is only one God and now he was to get a new blessing. As he entered the home of Peter in Jerusalem Paul turned to him and asked,

"Did you bring the change of clothes?"

Gabe was in his fighting outfit, it was a black outfit that he had gotten when he was done learning how to sword fight in the East. He also had a hooded cape that went with it to hide his face; he felt that it intimidated evil. Gabe looked at Paul,

"Yes I do..."And handed the normal clothes to him. Peter then spoke up,

"Good, now come with me."

Peter led Gabe to another room. In that room were two large bowls. To Peter's left was one of the large bowls, this one was full of water. Peter had rolled up his sleeves when he approached. Paul helped Gabe lean in over the bowl and then Peter said,

"I baptize you in the name of the Father and of the Son and of the Holy Ghost." He poured water over his head with each name he said and then Paul helped him to stand straight. Peter dipped his hand in the water and sprinkled some of it on his clothes saying, "I bless these clothes. Gabriel, you will not only fight evil but from this day forward you will be the protector of God's Church on Earth. Do you accept this responsibility?"

"I do with an open heart and mind."

"Then show me your palms." Peter dipped his fingers into some oil and then said as he made the sign of the cross on his palms, "From this day forward the outfit that you have on now will only appear when evil is nearby or you request it."

Even though the oils were cold two crosses burned into his palms when Peter was done making the sign. Gabe let out a scream and bent over as the pain from the burning hit him, but as fast as it came it was gone. He straightened himself again and Paul spoke up,

"Hand me your swords."

Gabe drew his swords and handed them to Paul. Paul and Peter went over to another large bowl full of oil, the same oil that they used to bless his palms, and dipped the sword into it. When they pulled them out two crosses glowed white on the base of the swords next to the hilt. They walked back up to Gabe and then handed his swords back to him. Gabe put them away and Peter told him,

"Now, from this point on, your outfit and your sword will appear, just as you have them now, whenever you need them. When you leave this room your outfit will disappear and you will be able to wear normal clothes."

Paul led him out of the room and when he crossed the threshold into the next room his clothes disappeared. Gabe grabbed the clothes that he brought with him and put them on. He looked at Paul,

"Now I know why God wanted me to bring this other outfit."

Paul smiled at him as Peter walked out into the room. Peter went up to him.

"May our Lord Jesus Christ be with you Gabriel."

"Thank you, Peter. I hope I get the chance to see you again.

Peter put his right hand on Gabe's shoulder, smiled, "No Gabriel, this is the last time you will see the both of us."

Gabe gave him a strange look and then said, "I am sure that we will see each other again. I come around here a lot."

"But we won't be here too much longer. Don't worry Gabriel, everything will be okay. But you need to be getting a going again."

Gabe smiled at them and walked out of the house.

Present Day

Gabe woke up from the dream. He sat up in his bed, looked at the time, it was two in the morning and then remembered, *That was the last time I saw them.*

Later that morning, Rebecca woke up to the sound of Gabe walking around upstairs. She got up and went to the kitchen where Gabe was sitting, eating breakfast. Gabe looked at her; she was still in her pajamas which were a tank top and shorts. He smiled,

"So how was your night?"

She smiled at him, "Good and you will be happy to know that all the bugs in the basement are now dead."

"Well did you want something to eat?"

"Yes, what do you have?" Rebecca walked up to the box of cereal that was on the table and saw that it was Luck Charms. She looked at him, "You eat kid's cereal?"

"Yes, why?"

"You fight all kinds of evil beings and you eat kid's cereal."

"Yep... Did you want some?"

"Sure, why not." Rebecca let out a little chuckle as Gabe got up and got a bowl and spoon out for her. He put the bowl on the table and got out the milk and put it in front of her. She fixed herself the bowl and then sat down to eat it. While she was eating,

"Did you think about going back last night?" Hoping that he had changed his mind.

"Look, Rebecca. . . I have been out of practice for such a long time. I will be just in the way."

"That is okay, we can practice right here. We will spare each other in the back. What do you think?"

"Boy, you have an answer for everything don't you?" Rebecca nodded her head as she chewed on some cereal. Gabe continued, "Look, I have a lot to do, why don't we talk more about this when I come back for lunch?"

Rebecca swallowed the food before speaking, "Okay, but we really need to talk about it Gabe. I need an answer soon, like now."

Gabe smiled, picked up his bowl and took it over to the sink. He then walked back to Rebecca,

"When you are done, just put your bowl in the sink and put the cereal and milk away, if you don't mind?"

"Sure... Not a problem."

Rebecca watched as Gabe walked out of the house and to the Quonset where a John Deere was sitting in front of it. She finished her cereal and after she put the stuff away she went down and got ready for the day.

Later on that morning, Rebecca was walking around the house. She was bored from waiting for Gabe to get back. The house is a nice sized brick ranch style house; She saw pictures and paintings, some of the farm and other sceneries and of Gabe during the many years of his work with the Vatican. She went into his office and saw a walk in closet. The door was open so she walked in. It had a lot of clothes that Gabe wore throughout the ages. In the back was another set of clothes, but these didn't look like normal clothes. She was very surprised to see what she found.

CHAPTER 9

REVOLUTION

Gabe had been out in the field all morning and was getting hungry. He had forgotten all about Rebecca and the request that the Vatican wants him back. But when he pulled into the yard and saw the black Buick it all came back to him. He pulled the tractor up to the gas tank next to the Quonset, turned it off and then went in. When he walked in the house and called out,

"Rebecca? Did you want to go get something to eat?"

From the office he could hear her respond, "Yah, sure… Where do you want to go?"

Gabe suddenly realized where the sound of her voice was coming from, that she was not only in his office, but in his walk in closet. He walked to his office and looked into the closet and there she was,

"What are you doing in here?"

"I was bored and decided to look around the house. I am a little shocked though."

"Why is that?"

"Well for someone that wanted to get away from fighting, it seems that you have gotten yourself in more wars over here." Rebecca pointed to the Revolutionary War uniform. Gabe cleared his throat,

"Look, sometimes when you see injustice you have to stand and fight against it."

"So that explains the Revolutionary Uniform and the blue Civil War Uniform, but what about the War of 1812 Uniform?"

34

"I saw the same threat that I saw in 1775 and I was not going to allow that to happen."

"But you said that you have been out of practice for too long, it doesn't look too long to me."

"I didn't do much in that kind of fighting except fire a musket and then charge the enemy. What you are asking me to do is go back to fighting with my swords and I just have not done that in such a long time, that I would be in the way. Now are you hungry or not."

"Okay, okay… Well where did you want to go to eat?'

"I was thinking about Burger King. We can go to that 'BIGGER' town across the river."

"Sounds good to me." Rebecca smiled and walked out of the closet.

That evening the two sat in the living room. The T.V. was on, but they paid no attention to it. Gabe was telling stories of past battle and Rebecca was just eating them up. She sat across from Gabe with her elbow on the armrest of the couch and holding her head up by her chin and Gabe sat relaxed in his easy chair. The grandfather clock started to chime and they both looked at it. It was nine o'clock at night and Gabe wanted to get some rest,

"Wow, is it that late already, well I am going to go to bed. I got more fields to do tomorrow. I'll be done with cultivating that field then."

"Well... Since you will be done with that, how about taking some time off and go with me to the Vatican."

"You don't give up easily, do you?"

"Nope...

"We will talk more tomorrow, how about that?"

Rebecca was getting a little antsy and wanted to go now, but she also felt that if she pushed too hard, Gabe would almost kick her out.

"Okay, we will talk tomorrow."

The next morning was the same routine. This time after Gabe left, Rebecca wanted to play on the pool table. She had seen it yesterday when she walked back and forth to her room. She found the pool balls and chalk, but couldn't find the queue sticks. As she looked around she saw a doorway that had a curtain in front of it. She went over to it, pulled back the curtain and instead of finding the queue sticks she found something else more interesting.

YES MASTER YODA.
SEE, LOGIC AND KNOWLEDGE CAN COME FROM ANYWHERE.

CHAPTER 10

THE WORK IS NEVER DONE

Father Scott walked into the rectory, the dishes needed to be done, floor vacuumed, bedroom cleaned and the laundry needed to be washed, but he had other things on his mind. He had just gotten back from Lincoln, Nebraska, he spent all day yesterday talking with the Bishop and the Bishop had a very special request of him. It took all day for the Bishop to explain what he needed to be done and why. After he put down his bags he sat down on the couch for a moment. On the stand next to the couch was his answering machine, the light was blinking that there were messages. Father leaned over and pushed play, the machine had about four messages about getting High School ready for the next school year. Some of the congregation had left him messages, one about a Baptism that he was going to do in a couple of days, another was just seeing how he was doing and inviting him over for supper tonight. Father looked up at the clock and saw that it was about eleven thirty. Knowing that he had to do something, he reluctantly got up and thought to himself, *take a shower first and then back to business*. He headed upstairs to freshen up.

Rebecca stood there amazed at the sight, but there is was, on a stand were two swords just like his other ones. She picked up the swords and got a good look at them. They were not made of silver and they looked like they have been used just recently, practice sword she thought. They were connected side by side. Rebecca thought to herself that Gabe must keep his swords like this normally. Then she thought for a moment, if these have been used then there must be a place that he practices in. She quickly ran outside with the swords and looked around the backyard for a place that he might have set up for practice. To her right was the Quonset and three grain bins behind that. In front of her was an open yard and after that is a large grouping of trees that ran all the way around the yard, but no visible practice area. Then it hit her, she saw a path into the tree, followed the path and there it was. She put the swords down on a stump and ran back in.

Gabe had finished the field that he was working on and it was time for lunch. This time he was thinking about the conversation he had with Rebecca last night, more like the stories that he told her. She didn't do much talking about her experience. He drove back into the yard and parked the tractor. As he was walking to the house to see if Rebecca wanted to go get something to eat he heard from the trees,

"Gabe! I'm over here!"

She found my practice area, Gabe thought to himself. "What are you doing back there?"

"Come and find out."

He walked into the trees and saw Rebecca wearing a short Spandex top and shorts. Gabe had to take a double-take,

"The Vatican lets you wear that to practice in?"

"Well, they had no choice in the matter. I needed something that allows free movement like my fighting outfit and this was the only way I could see doing."

"And they just let you?"

"It did take some convincing, but in the end Cardinal Staff backed me up. But I do have a question for you."

"And that is?"

"You are going to go to confession for all of these lies, right?"

"Look, Rebecca, I had done that job for over two thousand years if you want it, you can have it, but I am done with it. Got it?"

Rebecca knew that if she tried to push after that comment, it would just turn Gabe away, so she decided to go to a different subject, "Okay.

Well if you don't mind, can you give me some pointers? Maybe we can spare each other?"

Gabe looked down; on a stump beside Rebecca were the two swords that he used to practice with. He then took a deep breath and then looked at Rebecca saying,

"I don't know..."

"Come on, it beats fighting dummies all the time." She paused for a moment waiting for an answer. When none came, she said, "I guess you are right, I would hate to see you get beat by a woman."

Gabe smiled at her; he knew that she was trying to get to his ego.

"Okay, but let's take this out to the open yard. That way we have room to get around." *Okay, so it worked,* Gabe thought to himself. He walked over to grab his swords and then walked in front of Rebecca out to the yard. Once out in the yard, Gabe sensed Rebecca take a lung at' him, He stepped to his right and allowed Rebecca to go past him. She quickly turned around to face Gabe, Gabe smiled,

"You didn't think that I was just going to let you win did you?"

"I'm hoping you won't."

She went after him again, but this time he blocked and twisted around and tripped her up. She got back to her feet just as fast as she fell and then Gabe swung around with his right sword. She blocked and tried to knock it out of his hands, but he blocked that with his left sword. She then came back at him, he blocked, pushing her sword to the left, he stepped out of the way and went with his swords in for a slash, but she blocked with her left sword. Gabe pushed off on her and she took a couple of steps away. Gabe smiled again,

"You are doing well, but you are anticipating. You need to feel not to anticipate."

"Yes, Master Yoda."

"See, wisdom can come from anywhere."

Rebecca went after him with a lunge and the fighting was on again.

Father Scott was driving into Gabe's farm and parked behind Rebecca's rental car and got out. Once he was out he could hear something going on in the back yard. He ran to the back and to his surprise Gabe and Rebecca were fighting each other, but they had smiles on their faces, so Father understood that they were sparing each other and not engaged in actual battle. He was amazed at the level of skill that the two were showing. He didn't say a word, just leaned against the corner of the house and quietly watched.

The two were starting to go faster and faster. Soon it was getting hard to even see their swords move. Gabe was impressed with the level of skill that Rebecca was showing. Rebecca swung her sword towards Gabe's head, he took a knee. She then went down with both of her swords, Gabe blocked by making an X with his swords.

"Give up, I got the upper hand." Rebecca told him.

"You think so?"

Gabe slid her swords to his right, twisted around and connected his left leg with the back of her knees, she fell back on to the ground, Gabe swung around again, knocking her swords out of her hands, he jammed his sword into the ground next to her on each side and he pinned her down by holding her shoulders with his hands. A look of shock came over her face, he had done that so quickly that she didn't even see him move. Gabe smiled and stared into her eyes,

"You were saying?"

Rebecca didn't say anything, she was too shocked that Gabe could move that fast, but then they found themselves staring at each other. Their hearts started to pound a little harder. All of a sudden, they heard Father Scott clear his throat. The two jumped up, their faces red as a stop sign and they looked like children that had just been caught with their hands in the cookie jar. Father busted out laughing at seeing the two. Gabe spoke up first,

"Father... Ah. . . Nice to see you."

"Gabe, calm down. I was just amazed at you two. You reminded me of seeing an action movie."

"So Father, you came all the way out here just to say hi?"

"Yes and no. . . You two left in such a hurry on Monday that I was wondering if everything is okay."

"Everything is fine Father, you can tell that to the Bishop when he calls again."

"So where are you from Rebecca?"

"I'm from Denmark."

"And now you work for the Vatican."

"Yep… Been doing that for many years now."

"Okay, so how long are you planning on being here Rebecca?"

"Well, I am due back at the Vatican by Friday of next week."

"Good, then I can expect you two for mass this weekend?"

"We will be there Father." Gabe replied.

"Well good, I will see you two then."

"See you then Father."

With that Father Scott walked back to his car. The two watched as he drove away. Then the two turned to each other and laughed at the situation. Then a look of revelation came over Rebecca's face, so Gabe inquired,

"What is the matter?"

"I just remembered, I didn't pack any clothes for Mass."

"How can you forget to pack clothes for Mass?"

"I didn't think that it would take this long to convince you to come back. I thought that the moment you heard that the Vatican was in trouble you would have come back from that."

Gabe let out a sigh and then said, "Okay, we will go into town tomorrow and get you something to wear for Mass. How does that sound?"

"Sounds good, where are we going?"

"We'll go to J.C. Penny."

"Okay, well I am hungry, so let's go and get something to eat."

"That sounds good to me."

CHAPTER 11

A DRESS

Gabe drove Rebecca to the bigger city the next day so that she could found an outfit to wear for Mass on Sunday. On the way there Rebecca didn't say anything about going back to the Vatican with her. She didn't want to push the subject too much and from this point on she was going to enjoy her time off. At the store, Rebecca was having a hard time finding an outfit to wear. After about an hour of her trying different suits and dresses and asking Gabe what he thought about, Gabe was getting a little tired. Rebecca came out wearing a blue dress,

"What do you think about this one?"

"That one looks nice on you."

"I don't know..." Rebecca was looking at herself in the mirror, "I think it makes me look fat."

Gabe let out a sigh and mumbled, "Now I remembered one of the reasons I never remarried."

"What is that supposed to mean?" Rebecca responded harshly.

"Look... This is what, the tenth outfit you have tried on and five of them I said that I liked on you and you put them back."

"But I want to look good for Mass."

"Do you think that I would lie to you? Let's get that pin-striped suit and skirt. I think it would look best for Mass"

"But that one made me look tall."

"Rebecca. . . You're five foot seven inches, you are tall. I don't think it will matter what dress you get."

"Fine... You go get the suit and I will change and get the nylons."

Gabe went and grabbed the suit from the rack and took it up to the checkout counter. Gabe smiled at the cashier as she asked,

"Will that be all Gabe?"

"No, she is bringing nylons Mary"

Since he had shopped there many times, he knew almost everyone that worked there and they knew him.

"What kind of shoes is she getting?"

"Do you think she will need shoes?"

"This is your first time shopping for a female, isn't it?"

"Is it that obvious?"

Mary smiled at him, "I will go and get shoes that will work with this suit." As she was leaving the counter she turned to Gabe and said, "Oh... Gabe... You picked a good one. You two look great together."

"What?" Gabe was shocked at the comment, "Oh... Ha... We are not dating." But Mary didn't listen; she just kept walking to the shoe section.

Outside the store, Gabe and Rebecca were walking to the car. Rebecca told Gabe,

"Gabe... You know you didn't have to pay for my dress. I do have money you know."

"Consider it a gift. I was just shocked that Mary knew your shoe size just by looking at you."

"She is good at her job."

"That she is..."

After they got back in the car and were driving away, Gabe asked,

"Rebecca? Are you this indecisive in battle?"

"What do you mean?" Rebecca was taken back from the question.

"Well, it took you over an hour to find a dress for Mass. I am just hoping that you are not that indecisive in battle."

"No, I am not that indecisive in battle. I can make battle decisions when I needed to. In fact, I have made many quick decisions in the middle of battle."

"Well, I am glad to hear that. But may I make a suggestion? To make it easier for you in battle, practice it in your everyday life when you don't have to make a quick decision."

Rebecca folded her arms and looked out the window. Gabe drove over the viaduct and pulled on to a street. Rebecca asked,

"Where are we going?"

Gabe didn't say anything; he pulled the car up to a Dairy Queen drive through the window operator asked,

"Welcome to Dairy Queen. What can I get for you?" Gabe looked at Rebecca,

"What do you want?"

"Are you sure that I can handle deciding on ice cream?"

"What do you want?"

"M & M Blizzard please."

Gabe turned to the microphone and said, "Can I get an M & M Blizzard and a cherry dipped cone please?"

"Is that all for you?"

"Yes it is."

"Okay your total is six seventy five. Pull around to the window please."

"Thank you..."

Gabe pulled the car around and paid the cashier. She handed the ice cream to Gabe and Gabe handed them to Rebecca. After driving away Rebecca asked,

"Is this your way of saying that you are sorry?"

"Is it working?"

"Yes. . . How are you getting to know me so well?"

"Well, you have been around my farm for the last three days. People will start to get to know each other, even after a short while."

"That is true."

Later on that night Gabe was talking to Rebecca in the living room, he looked down at her hands,

"I have been noticing that you don't have any crosses burned into your hands. Did you get the same blessing as I did?"

"They tried, but the crosses wouldn't burn into my palms."

"But you will not die if you are shot right?"

"Actually, if I am stabbed in the heart or shot in the heart then I will die; I am not like you Gabe. I can be killed. I will live until the second coming of Christ as you can tell, but only if I am not stabbed or shot in the heart."

"So you can be killed."

"Yes, I can."

"Well, I don't broadcast it, but I can be killed as well. It's just a lot harder than simply shooting or stabbing me in the heart." Gabe smiled, "Now you said that you went after the Fang once already, but it was a disaster. Tell me a little bit about that."

"Well, the whole thing started two years ago. A Russian nuclear disposal was broken into and then last year Father Burns was found dead just outside the Vatican. He had a piece of paper in his hand that identified that it was a vampire group that stole the nuclear components. We got the Intel that it was the Fang that stole it in January this year and that the new leader, we don't know who it is, is planning on using it to blow up the Vatican. Two months ago we went in thinking that it was not going to be much of a fight. Like you said, they work in small groups. But what we found was a large group and this new well-trained guard. I was shot in the leg and took a knife stab in my arm. My assistant Mike picked me up and carried me to the landing zone. Once there, Mike put me down on the beach to help get the boats ready when one of the human minions shot him in the heart. When he fell dead, Colonel Curtis came and grabbed him and me and put us in the boats. It took me a month to recover from that. Unlike you Gabe, it takes me a lot longer to heal. That is when the Vatican decided to have me go and get you."

"So you know what went wrong?"

"We didn't get good Intel."

"Now you know what to expect and the way you and I spared, I know you can stop them."

"You are still trying to find a reason not to come back, aren't you?"

"Rebecca, I got tired of all of that. Everyone around you dying and you remain the same. They die in combat or they die of old age, it didn't make a difference. God gave me a blessing and in a way a curse at the same time. I am still tired of that, I really don't want to go back to doing that again."

Rebecca couldn't disagree with that. She smiled at him,

"Well... I'm not planning on going anywhere and I hope we are friends, right?"

"Yes... Of course, we are friends, but you can be killed and I just can't watch that happen again."

Rebecca stood up, walked over to Gabe, knelt in front of him and smiled.

"You can protect me. I know you could after the sparing that we have been doing."

Gabe returned the smile, "Let's not talk about this right now. I have one more field to do tomorrow and I want to get it done before it rains."

"Okay..."

Rebecca got up and walked to the couch to watch the show on the television. Gabe got up and went into his room to get some sleep.

CHAPTER 12

ROME A.D. 580

The sun was shining over Rome early in the morning. Gabe's new apartment had a direct view of Saint Peter's Basilica, right from his bedroom window. Gabe stood in front of the window enjoying the view. All at once, the ground began to shake, bricks started to fall from the building and cracks began to form in the streets below. Gabe held on to the window frame to steady himself. He kept looking out at the Basilica. Then to his shock, the Basilica started to collapse. In turning around, he found his own room crumbling around him. He quickly looked back out and all of Rome was falling in ruins, just as his apartment started to fall to the ground.

Present Day

Gabe woke up, jumping from a dead sleep. His breathing was heavy; sweat was running down his face and heart racing. Gabe ran his hands over his face wiping away the sweat. His heart was racing so fast that it took a few minutes for him to get a grasp on everything. Once he calmed down and happy to know that it was all a bad dream, he got up from his bed to get a drink. When he opened the door to his room he could hear the television going in the living room, Gabe went into the living room to find Rebecca sound asleep on the couch. She was in her tank top and shorts pajamas and looked cold. He went into the hallway closet and pulled out a blanket for her, went back in, laid the blanket over her, tucked it in a little and pushed away some of her red hair from her face. Gabe stood over her just for a moment, she looked very peaceful which made Gabe smile. The grandfather clock began to chime, Gabe turned around to see the time. It was two fifteen in the morning. He grabbed the remote out of Rebecca's hand, turned off the television and went and got himself something to drink. Gabe took one more look at Rebecca on his way back to his room to make sure she was okay and then went to bed.

About seven that morning, Gabe was in the kitchen eating breakfast. Rebecca woke up, wrapped herself up in the blanket, walked into the kitchen to see Gabe eating,

"Did you get the blanket for me last night?"

"Yeah… I woke up around two and saw you on the couch. You looked cold so I got it out of the closet in the hall."

"Well thank you, but why didn't you wake me up?"

"You looked too comfortable."

"Well, your couch is very comfortable. So what are you going to do today?"

"I got one more field to finish up today."

"Oh… Okay… I guess I can go out back and practice while you are gone."

Gabe gave her an inquisitive look and asked, "Did you want to come along?"

A look of shock came over Rebecca's face, and then she asked, "Really? Are you sure I won't be in the way?"

"Of course not… I'll even let you drive the tractor, besides it beats sitting around here being bored the whole time."

"Okay! Sure!" Rebecca was excited, she had never worked on a farm before and so this was going to be something new to her,

"Well run down and get changed out of your pajamas and I will wait for you here."

"Okay…" She took off downstairs to get ready. When Gabe heard the shower turn on, he went downstairs to the bathroom door, knocked,

"What are you doing?"

"Getting ready, why?"

"Rebecca you're going to get dirty in the field, don't take a shower until you are done with work."

"Oh… Yah… Your right…" She turned the shower off, Gabe headed back upstairs to wait for her. When Rebecca was back upstairs, Gabe smiled at her and shook his head. She gave him a strange look,

"What???"

"Taking a shower?"

"I always take a shower when I get ready; I've never worked on a farm before."

"That I would believe…"

The two went out to the Quonset and got the tractor ready. Gabe drove to the field that he needed to work on. He drove for the first two rounds and then he turned to Rebecca,

"So. . . Do you want to give it a try?"

"I don't know…"

"It's easy, just go down the rows like you have seen me do and just don't take out any crop, that's your profit."

"No pressure though, right?"

"No, not at all…"

"I don't know…"

"Here…" Gabe pushed the seat back as far as it could go and lowered the steering wheel all the way down. Then he said, "Sit right here," Pointing in front of him, "I'll work the pedals, the gears and the hydraulics. All you have to do is steer, if there is any problem I'll be right here."

Rebecca gave him an inquisitive look, then Gabe said, "Oh… come on, you know that I'm not going to try anything; I'm the one person you can trust in this matter and besides, we are both adults here. My right hand and feet are going to be too busy working the tractor, the only arm that is going to be touching you is my left to hold you up, come on."

"Okay..." Rebecca went over, sat in front of Gabe, Gabe put his feet on either side of Rebecca to push on the pedals, his left arm went around Rebecca holding her up by her waist and he put his right hand on the gear shift. He looked over Rebecca's right shoulder and asked,

"Ready to go?"

"I guess..." She grabbed the wheel; Gabe put the tractor in gear, dropped the cultivator and released the clutch.

As they started down the field, Gabe noticed that Rebecca was a little nervous; she gripped the steering wheel like her life depended on it. Gabe chuckled,

"Relax you're doing just fine."

"Are you sure?"

"You haven't taken out any corn yet, so yes."

Rebecca began to relax until they got close to the end of the field. She looked at Gabe and asked,

"Ah... Gabe, what do you want me to do?"

"Keep going straight, I'll stop the tractor."

Soon they were at the end of the field, Gabe was not stopping and Rebecca was getting really nervous, Gabe wasn't even slowing down, so Rebecca closed her eyes,

"Uh... Gabe... Gabe... Gabe!!!"

CHAPTER 13

SATURDAY

Rebecca peeked out at what happened. Gabe stopped the tractor inches from the fence. Rebecca was breathing heavy, she looked back at Gabe, hit his shoulder,

"Ouch! What was that for?"

"You scared the living daylights out of me!"

"You??? You who fight evil of all kinds got scared of this?"

"Well… Why didn't you stop until now?"

"I had to bring the cultivator all the way through the field." Gabe pointed behind himself.

Rebecca looked back and sure enough the cultivator was sitting just at the end of the field. Gabe lifted the cultivator and the tractor rolled backward just a little bit. Then Gabe backed up the tractor a little bit more so that there was enough room to turn the tractor, then he said,

"Okay, Rebecca… Turn the steering wheel left until it won't turn anymore."

Rebecca started to slowly turn the wheel and turned it and turned it and turned it. Finally, she asked,

"How far do you want me to turn this?"

"Until you can't turn it anymore… Grab the knob on the wheel and use it to spin the wheel until it stops."

Rebecca began to spin the wheel and when it finally stopped, "Okay, it's done."

Gabe put the tractor in gear, released the clutch and pressed down on the left brake. The tractor turned sharply. When the tractor was straight along the end of the rows,

"Okay, straighten the wheel."

Rebecca straightened the wheels and as they were going along the rows Gabe counted them until he got to seven, he stopped and said, "Okay Rebecca, turn left again."

Rebecca spun the wheel around again and Gabe pushed on the left brake too sharply turn the tractor straight with the rows. Rebecca straightened the wheels again, Gabe dropped the cultivator and they were off again going down the rows.

They spent the rest of the day going through the field, stopping only for a few minutes to eat. Gabe talked about the many times he hit the fence or came across problems while in the field, or they would tell each other jokes to pass the time. When they were done, Rebecca drove the tractor back to the yard and they went inside. Inside the house,

"So do you want to go to a Steak House to get something to eat?"

"That sounds good."

"Well, get changed and this time you can take a shower."

"Are you sure?"

"Yes... You now have my permission."

"Oh... Thank you."

Gabe smiled at her as she walked downstairs. After supper at the Steak House; Gabe and Rebecca finished the night talking in the living room. Again Rebecca wanted to hear about the battles that Gabe was in.

The next morning Rebecca asked Gabe as they were eating breakfast,

"So, since you are done with the fields, do you think you can come back with me to the Vatican?"

"Rebecca... that is not the only thing that needs to be done on a farm; that is just one out of many things that needs to be done. Besides, I have not fought since the Civil War, fighting has changed. I am not used to the new weapons, like the rifles and pistols."

"What??? That is not what the people say here in Williamsville. In fact, they say you can put round on top of round. That you once shot a deer that no one saw except you."

"What did you do? Go around asking people what kind of a hunter I am?"

"No… To tell you the truth, once I said your name, boy did the stories started, good and bad. They just seemed to talk about you and they didn't even give me your address, all they did is talk about the last hunting outing they had with you."

Gabe put his head down, ran his hands over his face and responded, "They are great people here, but sometimes they give a little too much information. Look I am not ready to decide right now and Father is expecting us at Mass."

"Okay… But I cannot wait for very long now. I wish you would just see the danger that the Vatican is in; that I need your help on this one."

Gabe didn't respond, he just looked away for a moment. Rebecca smiled at him. The rest of the day was spent outside sparing each other, and then they decided to go swimming at the Aquatic Center in the bigger city to cool off from the workout.

CHAPTER 14

SUNDAY

Early in the morning; Gabe was walking around the house. It was about eight thirty and Gabe wanted to get ready for Mass. He always made sure that he was ready to go long before he had to be. Rebecca came walking up and saw that this time Gabe was not at the table eating. He walked into the kitchen to see Rebecca still in her pajamas and asked,

"What are you doing? You need to get ready to go. Mass is at ten o'clock and I like to get there about half an hour early."

"Really... Why?"

"We do a Rosary before Mass starts and I like to be there for that."

"Okay, just give me a minute and I will be ready." Rebecca walked back downstairs and got ready for Mass.

At nine thirty Gabe and Rebecca pulled into the parking lot of Saint Peter's Church. They walked in and found their seats up front. After they knelt down for the Rosary Rebecca asked,

"Why do you sit up front?"

"Father asked me to, how could I say no to Father?"

"That is true..."

As the church started to fill up, Gabe could feel everyone looking his way, but he kept his focus on the Mass and not everyone else. During the homily, Father Scott talked about the importance of faith and reading the Bible. When Mass was over, everyone walked out to the front of the church to chat with Father and each other on things

55

that have been going on. A lot of them want to talk to Gabe especially. No one has ever seen him come to Mass with anyone and after seeing him in Mass with a female, they just had to know. While Rebecca was talking to Father Scott, one of them went up to Gabe,

"So Gabe??? Who is the nice lady that is with you today?"

"Her name is Rebecca Van Stocks and no, we are not dating."

"Really… You two seemed to be sitting pretty close together to not be dating?" Another responded.

"She is just a friend."

"Yah… We don't buy that Gabe. You may say that, but there is more going on than what you are telling us."

"Where is she from?" Tom asked

"She is from Rome."

"Really, why is she here in Nebraska?"

"Business…"

"What kind of business does she do?"

Gabe had to think for a moment and the best thing to say, without telling them completely what she does. "She is a messenger for the Vatican."

"Oh… Is she a nun?"

"No… Just a messenger."

"What kind of message does she have?"

"To tell everyone to keep their noses out of everyone else's business."

"Yeah… Okay, Gabe. We will just talk to Father and get the information from him."

"Go right ahead." Gabe knew that he couldn't tell them what Rebecca does, that he had sworn to secrecy. But a new thought was going through his head. Were they right? Are we sitting a little to close? Are we a little too friendly? Rebecca finished talking to Father Scott she went to Gabe,

"Are you ready, or did you want to stay a little longer to get drilled some more?"

"You heard that?"

"Who couldn't, I even had people come up to me and ask questions while I was trying to talk to Father."

"Well, I don't need any more questions, do you?"

"Nope, let's go."

They walked to the car and drove back to the house. Gabe, on the other hand, couldn't get the thoughts out of his head. He was very quiet on the way home and wasn't too talkative at home. They watched television for a while, and then went out to eat at Applebee's that evening. Gabe would talk to Rebecca a little here and there, but for the most part, he kept to himself.

CHAPTER 15

REBECCA

Gabe woke up from a bad dream, more like a memory. The day that Backular killed his whole family. He had a hard time falling back to sleep, so he got up and went into the kitchen to fix himself something to eat. It was about five in the morning and when Gabe looked out the window in front of the kitchen table he could see that clouds had rolled in last night and it was raining pretty well. He watched the rain come down and every so often there would be lightning flash, followed by the roar of thunder. The trees would sway as small gusts of wind would pick up, pushing the rain to one side or another, like waves in the ocean. Gabe was happy that he got his current fieldwork done before the rain came. That meant that he could completely enjoy the day off this Monday. He sat down at the table with a bowl of Trix and started to eat while at the same time watching the rain come down.

About six thirty-five there was a loud crash of thunder that woke Rebecca up. She looked around for a moment to get a sense of what was going on. When she realized that it was a thunderstorm she looked at the time, then got up. The room was a little chillier than normal so she grabbed one of the blankets off the bed and then went upstairs. When she got to the kitchen she looked out the window. The sun was up, but the dark stormy clouds made it look like night time. She looked at Gabe as he said,

"I was wondering if that last crash of thunder would wake you up."

"How long has it been raining?"

"For a while now."

"Well... I'm glad to see that you are talking to me again. You didn't say much after Mass yesterday. Did I do something wrong?"

"No Rebecca... You have not done anything wrong." Rebecca walked over and took a seat beside Gabe and then he continued, "No... I... I just... I had something on my mind."

Rebecca stared at him trying to get him to say what the problem was, instead he asked,

"So how did you come to work for the Vatican?"

"Well... That is a long story."

"Well... According to the weather, we have plenty of time." Gabe pointed outside.

"Okay... then, it all started.

Frankfurt Germany A.D. 1930

A couple was walking along through a park, holding each other's hands and smiling at each other. Rebecca had a bag on her shoulder; she had just got done with dance class. She was performing ballet at her school. The male with her was about five foot ten inches, had dark brown hair and blue eyes. When they came to a park bench he stopped and asked,

"Say, do you remember this spot?"

Rebecca looked down at the bench, "Somewhat, why?"

"Well, this was the place where we first met."

She looked again, "You're right... You remember that?"

"How can I forget, but to make sure you'll never forget..."He got down on one knee, reached into his pocket, pulled out a box and opened it and asked, "Rebecca Van Stocks, will you marry me?"

She dropped her bag, was having a hard time breathing but managed to say, "Yes... Yes, Johnny... Of course, I will."

John stood up, pulled out the ring, put it on her finger and kissed her. She looked at him,

"Let's get back to my apartment, there is a phone downstairs, we need to tell my parents."

"No need…"

"No need??? Why not???"

"Because… I called your father to get permission two days ago. Your parents already know and are here in Frankfurt along with mine. They are waiting for us at the restaurant to celebrate our engagement."

"Boy… You thought of everything, didn't you?"

"Yes, I did…"John smiled at her, he knew that impressed her.

They first went to her apartment to drop off her bags and to change clothes. Then they walked to the restaurant. As they were walking the two talked about the plans for the wedding. Paying no attention to what was going on around them and when they turned the corner to head down the restaurant they found themselves right in the middle of a battle. One of them yelled out,

"Get out of here!!!"

But it was too late. The second man, a tall muscular man with white hair turned to them and quickly ran over. He first went after John stabbing him in the heart. John fell backward landing on Rebecca and pushing her up against a brick wall. She panicked and tried to push John's body off of her, but as soon as she was free the tall man was ready to attack her, she froze and felt that she couldn't move at all. Just before he was able to stab her, the one that yelled out at them jumped in front of the sword. She could see the sword sticking out of his chest as he fell to his knees. The tall man attacking them looked at her. His smile and almost white eyes sent chills up and down her body as if someone had put her in a freezer. He pushed the man's body against her and the two slid to the ground. They both heard the whistles of the police officers come to her aid. The tall man looked at the officer running down the street, then back at her and gave her one more chilling smile. Once he took off running, Rebecca looked around at John's dead body and this man that sacrificed himself dying in her arms. His breathing was getting shallower. A necklace was visible, so she picked it up, hoping to get maybe a name for him, but instead, she saw a symbol that she saw once on her trip to the Vatican two months ago. She held it in her hand for a moment when he looked up at her and whispered,

"Take it…"

She leaned in to hear him better and whispered, "I'm sorry?"

"Take it… It is yours now. You are the one that…"And with that, he let out his last breath.

Before the police arrived she took it off of him and put it in her pocket. The officers helped her up and had her stand off to the side as the police and medics checked out John and the other guy. One of them went up to her and asked,

"Did you know these men?"

"That… That one is John, but I don't know the other one."

Minutes later the officer helped the medics put the covers over the body and put them in the cart, one of the officers went up to her,

"Are you okay? Did you want to come down to the station?"

"No… I have to go tell his parents."

"We can do that madam."

"NO… I must tell them!"

"Very well madam, this is the hospital that they can go to." He handed her a piece of paper and walked away.

"Thank you…" He turned around and smiled at her.

When everyone was gone she broke down and started to cry. Her clothes soaked with Johnny's and the other man's blood. After a few minutes, she pulled out the necklace, squeezed it in her hand, got up and walked down the street to the restaurant.

At the restaurant, John and Rebecca's parents were waiting at the table for the two to show up. Finally, Rebecca's father saw her walk in.

"There's my little girl." He said.

All four of them stood up to see Rebecca walk in by herself. The look on her face and the blood on her clothes gave everyone chills. Her mother ran up to her,

"Rebecca? What is the matter? Where is John?"

She looked at John's parents; she didn't know what to say, so she just shook her head. A look of concern came over their faces and his mother asked,

"Where's my Johnny?!"

"I'm sorry... We were on our way here when..." She handed the piece of paper to his father, his mother started to cry and put her face into her husband's chest. He put one hand on his wife and the other hand on Rebecca's shoulder.

"Did you want to come with us to the hospital?"

Rebecca shook her head and said, "I'm sorry, I can't see him right now."

"It's okay, I understand." He helped his wife outside. Rebecca's parents went and comforted her.

CHAPTER 16

RAINY DAY

"After the funeral, I went to Rome. I swore from that day on I was going to get Backular. I promised myself that I would never freeze like that again and that I was going to take over Brian's job."

"Not to sound heartless by not talking about John, but they gave my job to Brian?"

"Did you know him?"

"I met him once. He was a brass new recruit with a lot of ambition when I left over two hundred years ago."

"So now you know why I took the job."

"That I do… Did you tell your parents what you were doing?"

"They had this strange notion that I became a nun."

"So in other words… No…"

"I didn't think my mother would be able to handle the fact of me fighting."

"I can see that. Well, today is going to be sit-around-the-house-in-pajamas day. This rain is going to last all day."

"Is that what the weatherman says?"

"The weatherman and Farmer's Almanac…"

"Farmer's Almanac???"

"When you live on a farm, you get to know how to read the weather. They call it the Farmer's Almanac."

Gabe got up from the table, Rebecca made herself some breakfast. After breakfast, they sat around the house in their pajamas all day as the

63

rain continued to fall. The rain would calm down every so often, but then it would pick up again right away. As night began to fall, the storm seemed to get worse. Gabe and Rebecca made themselves a picnic on the floor of the living room, where they could watch the storm and every so often watch the television. When one lightning struck the power went out. Gabe got up and lit some candles, put them around the picnic area and sat down again next to Rebecca. He smiled at her,

"You know Rebecca… this picnic idea of yours was a great one."

"Well thank you, I'm glad you are enjoying it."

Gabe continued to tell stories of the past and Rebecca just listened intently. Suddenly they hear a loud crash of thunder; Rebecca jumped, grabbed a hold of Gabe and put her head into his chest. She then looked up at Gabe; they stared at each other for a moment. Their hearts began to race and faces started to turn red. When Gabe felt all of this, he took a deep breath, got up and walked out of the room into the bathroom to splash water on his face. Rebecca watched him as he left, she bit her bottom lip and then looked down when he was out of sight.

AND THERE IS
NO WAY I CAN
CHANGE YOUR
MIND?

CHAPTER 17

WHAT IT TAKES

The sun was coming up; Gabe sat at the table, but didn't have any food. It was a beautiful day, but Gabe didn't feel good at all. He wasn't sick, thoughts of his family and how close he was getting to Rebecca last night, the idea of getting close to her and having to see her die in battle was scaring him. He left the Vatican to get away from that, to get away seeing his best friends die and now he was getting a little too close to Rebecca for comfort, Rebecca came upstairs, she was rubbing her eyes,

"So how are you doing this morning Gabe?"

Gabe took a deep breath before he responded, "We need to talk Rebecca, have a seat."

Rebecca looked down, "I think I better stand, this doesn't sound good."

"Your choice... I have come to a final decision on going back and I..." Gabe paused for a moment and then continued, "I can't go back with you."

"Is it me? Have I done something wrong?"

"No... Oh no, Rebecca... heavens no... you have not done anything wrong. I just have too much to do here. I just can't leave the farm."

"I see, and there is no changing your mind?"

Gabe just shook his head; he couldn't say anything else from that. Rebecca turned away, she was trying to hold back her tears and she didn't want Gabe to see that. She cleared her throat,

"I guess that is all then."

She turned and walked back downstairs. Gabe wanted to say something, anything, but nothing was coming out. When he heard the shower turn on he decided to go and work on one of his pivot irrigation systems. He would talk to her more when he got back.

He was out in the far-field working on the systems. He couldn't get the look of Rebecca's face off his mind and it made it difficult to work. He worked for about an hour and then went back in. When he entered the yard, the black Buick was gone. Gabe's heart dropped to his stomach, he pulled the pickup to the garage, went inside and called out,

"Rebecca??? Are you here?"

But… As he knew it… there was no answer. He walked downstairs to the spare bedroom, turned on the light and her bags were gone. On the bed was the dress that he bought for her, but no note, nothing else was left. Gabe lowered his head trying to hold back the tears. He hurt all over as he turned around, walked up to the door, and before turning out the lights; he took one more look at the dress, turned out the lights, walked out and closed the door.

That afternoon Gabe was in his living room, it wasn't the same. It seemed empty, lonely and he just couldn't stand it. Just two weeks ago he was enjoying being by himself, but now it was killing him inside. He leaned back in his easy chair and it wasn't long before he fell asleep.

Gabe was running through some demons attacking him. He was calling out Rebecca's name as he was killing one demon after another. When he finally got within twenty feet to Rebecca, she was standing next to an exploded case. She smiled at him and it made Gabe calm down. He breathed a sigh of relief. A soldier was standing next him smiled,

"She is good at her job."

"That she is." Gabe responded.

Then all at once, three people possessed by demons came at him from his left, and three from his right. He reached across his body with both hands, pulled out two pistols and started to shoot at them, he looked to Rebecca and a demon came up from behind her, thrust a sword into her back. The blade stuck out of her chest. Gabe let out a yell,

"NO!!!"

Gabe jumped up from the easy chair, his heart pounding, almost felt as if it was about to pound out of his chest. He quickly got up and walked outside to get some air. He had never had such a bad dream that it made him feel like that.

It was evening and the sun was close to setting. He walked out onto the other side of the road, to watch the sun set. As he was looking onward, he saw something in the field in front of him. It looked as if some of the corn was not growing and some of it was dying. He walked out into the field and when he was closer he felt his clothes change, the swords appear behind him. He then remembered that Rebecca had thrown that pendent into the field. When he finally got to the spot, he bent down, uncovered the pendant, picked it up and then turned around. It was still covered in plastic, he looked at the road and saw Father Scott's car stopping on the side of the road. He walked up to Father,

"Father… good to see you. What are you doing here?"

"You know Gabe; I got this strange visit from Rebecca today."

"Really, what was strange about it?"

"Well… She told me that she was leaving for the Vatican tomorrow; she was going to stay at a hotel in Omaha tonight and leave in the morning. She said that you were not coming when I asked if you were and thanked me for helping her and then left. If I were to guess, she was almost in tears when she left. Do you know anything about that?"

Gabe looked down at the ground; he couldn't say anything for the first time in a long time. Father put his hand on his shoulder,

"Look, Gabe, I know that I have not been around as long as you, but I can say this. If you don't go back and she gets killed you will never forgive yourself. Your life will never be the same and you know very well. If the Fang is successful, the whole world will look like that field over there. You will have to get involved then and this time they will be too powerful for you to do anything. If you feel alone now, wait until you are the only human left on this earth."

Gabe looked back at the field; it was already beginning to come back. Then Gabe looked up at Father, took his gloves off, unwrapped the plastic from the pendant, laid it in his palm and it turned to ash in his hand. Father could see the crosses in his palms for the first time. He then asked Father,

"Father, I have a favor to ask of you."

CHAPTER 18

BACK TO ROME

Rebecca put her clothes into her suitcase, closed the lid and zipped it up. She walked to the window, looked out at Omaha, Nebraska, put her right hand on the frame and let out a sigh. After a minute or two she heard a knock on her door and the bell boy saying,

"Madam, your car is downstairs and ready when you are."

She walked to the door, opened it and replied, "Thank you, can you help me with my bags?"

The young bell boy walked in and grabbed two of her bags and walked out. Rebecca grabbed the other and followed him out. Downstairs the driver was standing by the car when he saw Rebecca come out of the hotel; he opened the door for her. She tipped the bellboy as he went to put the bags into the trunk. The driver drove Rebecca to the Omaha airport and right on the tarmac next to the plane. The driver got out, went around, opened the back passenger door and Rebecca stepped out. She looked up at the top of the steps to see the Captain waiting for her. The attendant for the plane got the bags out of the trunk and put them under the plane as Rebecca walked up the steps. When she got to the top the captain greeted her,

"Madam, we are of course ready when you are."

"Thank you, Captain." She turned to take one more look out at tarmac, hoping to see Gabe coming down saying that he had changed his mind and that he was coming along. She stood there for a moment, that is when the Captain asked,

"Madam, is everything all right?"

She took in a deep breath, looked at the skyline of Omaha and let it out,

"Yes Captain, everything is fine." But she didn't sound too convincing. She stepped into the plane and started to walk back to her normal seat. The Captain closed the door behind her. Rebecca walked past the command center and as she got to the conference room she could hear the troops that came with her talking among themselves. She couldn't make out what they were saying, but she really didn't care, her mind was not on what the troops were talking about. Suddenly she saw a figure lean over and say,

"You are late. What? Did you have a hard time finding something to wear?"

Rebecca's heart dropped, her eyes widened and she almost lost her balance. She grabbed ahold of the headrest of the first seat to steady herself. Finally, she managed to open her mouth,

"Well… You were not there to force a decision on me."

"You took off too quickly. You should have stuck around, I would have helped you out on that." She ignored that comment and asked,

"So? Why are you here?"

"You forgot your dress." Gabe pointed with his right thumb to something behind him. She looked up, and there it was hanging right behind him, wrapped in a plastic bag. She then looked down at him,

"Why didn't you just drop it off and then leave?" She wanted to see if she could get him to say something, that for some odd reason, she wanted to hear from him, but…

"Well, you see when I got here to drop off the dress. I thought to myself, I have come this far, I might as well get on the plane. I have never been on a plane this big before so I wanted to get on and see what it was like. Well after that, I thought, hey, since I am on the plane, I might as well get a ride. So I want up to the Captain and asked him if he could give me a ride around Omaha. Well, the Captain said that if I wanted a ride, I will have to go with them to Rome, because he doesn't just give free rides just around the area. So I guess I am heading to Rome with you."

"And when you get there, are you going to turn around and head back?"

"Well… Since I am going to Rome, I might as well stay and have a look around. It has been a long time since I have been there." He looked at Rebecca's face; she was giving him a "yeah, right" kind of look so he smiled at her and continued, "And see what I can do to help your little problem out."

"Are you sure you want to?"

"I can get up and go if you don't want me to help."

"Well… Since you are here, I guess I could use the extra help." Then she smiled at him.

"Then you better have a seat, I think the Captain wants to take off. You like the window seat right?"

"I love the window seat." Rebecca squeezed past Gabe and sat down next to him and the window. She looked over at the troops, that were still talking among themselves and then she looked back at Gabe,

"Do they know who you are?" Pointing to the troops sitting across from them.

"I have not told them yet. Why?"

"Hold on, when the plane is in the air, you will see."

The plane taxied down the runway, wait for their turn to take off. After a plane landed the Captain put the Vatican 747 in position and then took off. When they got to the flight level and the Captain turned off the seatbelt sign, Rebecca leaned over Gabe and got the troop's attention. One of them responded saying,

"Yes madam, what do you need?"

"Do you know who this is?"

"No… sorry madam."

"Gentlemen, I would like to introduce you to Gabriel. Gabriel, these are going to be some of your troops."

Silence filled the air as their jaws dropped. Rebecca looked at Gabe; smiled,

"I think we are going to have a nice flight."

Gabe looked at her as to say, why did you do that?

CHAPTER 19

SPEED IT UP

The sun was setting over the sea, creating a golden glow on the water with shimmers of light against the ripples on the ocean as twilights approach. How Melina wished she could see it with her own eyes, though she dared not to say anything. Steve walked up beside her to see the security camera. He had his hands in his pockets. He wasn't a tall man; he only stood about five foot seven inches. His dyed white hair gave him the look of age, even if it was fake. He had no scars, no deformities at all, he was born a vampire. Second generation, he would often remind people. Melina stepped away from the monitors and happy to do so. Steve was attracted to her and made no bones in letting her know. He would often probe her thoughts for one reason or another, but Melina didn't like him probing or have any interest in him or any man for that matter. So she would block her thoughts from him. It was a skill that she picked up many years ago and for some odd reason, Steve and a lot of the other vampires wouldn't block theirs. Either they just simply didn't want to, didn't know how or couldn't. But she had to work with Steve; he was her second in command in the Fang. The elders demanded that she make him her second since she was bitten and not one of the children of the elders or one of the elders. On top of that, she was only bitten five years ago in Berlin, but she gained rank fast and just a year and a half ago she climbed to the top spot. She could feel Steve turn around and was going to go up behind

74

her. She knew that he always likes to put his arm around her or grab her buttocks, but as soon as he turned around Jessica walked in saying,

"Melina madam, he is on the phone for you."

Saved by the bell, Melina thought, but then Steve chimed in,

"Who is on the phone Melina?" He folded his arms and waited for an answer, thinking that she had a boyfriend and didn't tell him.

"My contact from the Vatican, Steve. I have told you before that I have a contact in the Vatican and don't worry about probing Jessica's mind; she doesn't know who it is. This is how we stay one step ahead of the Vatican." Melina looked at Jessica, "I'll take it in my office."

"Yes, madam…"

A few minutes later she was in her office, picked up the phone,

"Yes, sir?"

"Melina… I just got word that Rebecca is on her way back. The last word was that she was not successful in ringing Gabriel back."

"So we don't have much to worry about."

"We still have to deal with the fact that they will be ready this time and with Rebecca coming back sooner than planned we will need to pick up the pace. Where is the case at right now?"

"We are getting close. The good doctor has said that he has a device that can hide the radiation, and the longest part now is building the device."

"Well, you need to tell him to hurry up."

"Yes, sir… It will be done and this time it will be done on time."

"You better hope so Melina."

"Yes, sir…"

"Call me when it is ready to go."

"Yes sir, will do sir."

The phone clicked off and Melina put the phone down. She went out to Jessica's desk,

"Get this message to Steve. I want him on that doctor every half hour now. Rebecca is heading back and it won't be long before they have a plan of attack. This time they will be ready for our Special Guard."

"Yes, madam, is there anything else?" "Just meet me in my room when you are done." "Yes, madam…" Jessica stood up and walked to the tunnels. Melina headed to her room, it had been some time since she had filled her blood thirst and she had a fresh bottle in her room.

Cardnal
Staff

<h1 style="text-align:center">CHAPTER 20</h1>

ROME

First Rebecca stepped out of the plane and the driver went and opened the door for her. She stepped down off the stairs to the plane with her dress in hand and walked up to the drive to get in the car. The driver was about to close the door when Rebecca spoke up,

"Hold on for a moment there."

"Madam???"

"Gabriel is talking to the troops; they won't stop asking him questions."

"Gabriel madam???"

"Yes… You know, Gabriel…" Rebecca looked up at the stairs and saw Gabe finally emerge. He looked down at Rebecca, shook his head and then went down the steps. When he got to the car he saw the driver with a look of shock on his face. Gabe got into the car and the driver shut the door behind him. He then got in and started to head to the Vatican. On the way, the driver kept looking back at Gabe. Noticing him Gabe spoke up,

"Is there a question that you have, sir?"

"Oh… N… No sir…" The driver stuttered, "I just thought that you would have been taller. I mean, all the stories that I have heard about you…"

"Yes… I seem to be getting that a lot lately and this is what I have told the others. Look when I was working for the Vatican, the average height of a man was five foot five inches tall. So to others, being that I am five foot nine inches tall, I was a tall man."

"That makes sense sir."

After about an hour of driving through traffic, they pulled up to Saint Peter's Square. It had been years since Gabe had seen the Square live and he wanted to walk through it. The two got out and the driver went up to Rebecca,

"I will take your bags to the apartment."

"Thank you, just leave them in the walkway."

The driver got back in the car and drove away. Gabe then asked,

"So do you have my old apartment?"

"As a matter of fact, I do."

"Well, I am glad that it is still being used then,"

They walked up to Saint Peter's Basilica. As they got close to the door of the Basilica Gabe saw a man trying to push a large trash cart, He was about Gabe's height, but a lot heavier and seemed to walk with a limp, he also looked a little ragged. So Gabe ran up to help him,

"Let me help you with that, sir."

"I got it!" He barked back at Gabe.

Gabe jolted back in shock; he thought that he would welcome the help. That is when he felt someone walking up behind him. He heard a voice speaking from behind,

"That is James Walker," Gabe turned around to see a man about six feet, grey hair, wearing glasses and in a Cardinal's black and red garb. The man continued, "He is hard to get along with sometimes, but he is a hard worker and he has a good heart at times."

"I can see that. Cardinal???"

"Cardinal Robert Staff and you are Gabriel; it is nice to meet you." He held out his hand to offer it to Gabe to shake. Gabe smiled and shook his hand,

"Yes… Rebecca has talked a lot about you in Nebraska. The pleasure it all mine."

"Well, you can't believe everything that she says. Except; of course, all the good things."

"Oh… So I can throw all of it out then." Gabe gave him a comical grin.

Rebecca hit him in the shoulder, Gabe looked at her,

"I guess it was all good. Unless of course, you are Matthew Duncan."

"Oh… Yes… He is waiting for us in the conference room, He wants to talk to you Rebecca and I can bet that now that you are here Gabriel, he will want to talk to you as well," Cardinal informed them.

"Well, I guess we better get a going then." Rebecca replied.

Cardinal Staff led them through the Vatican to one of the conference rooms. When Cardinal walked in he saw Matthew Duncan sitting in a chair. He looked over at the door, stood up when it opened,

"Cardinal, good is Rebecca with you?"

"Yes, she is…"

Then Rebecca walked in and right behind her was Gabe. Matthew saw Gabe, but didn't recognize him since he had never seen him before and was under the impression that Gabe was not coming so he asked,

"And who is this?"

"Matthew Duncan, this is Gabriel. Gabe this is Matt Duncan." Gabe walked up to Matt to shake his hand, but when he got to him, Matt put his hands behind his back,

"I thought that you weren't coming?"

"I changed my mind."

"Well, you should have never left in the first place. If you were here, we would not be in the mess that we are in now."

Gabe smiled at him, "You know what, you are right. If I had not left we would be in a lot better condition." He then looked at Rebecca, "There you go Rebecca. Matthew solved the whole problem, now we can go and enjoy the rest of my vacation here in Rome."

Gabe walked up to Rebecca, grabbed her hand and led her out of the conference room. Cardinal Staff gave Matthew a disapproving look and went after the two. Out in the hall, Cardinal stepped in front of Gabe,

"I am so sorry about that Gabriel."

"Why are you sorry, you have not disrespected me, Matthew has."

"Gabriel, I will control Matt. You have my word on that. We do need you though, there is more going on here than what we are seeing and I know that you can solve it,"

"I will do it if and only if, I am in charge of the whole mission. That is how it was done before I left and that is how I am going to do it now."

"I wouldn't have it any other way."

Gabe looked at Rebecca, gave her a smile, "Then what is the problem?"

"Let's go back in and talk to Matt. He has some information on the current problem with the Fang." They walked back into the conference room, Matt stood up again as they walked in, "Matt… Gabe is going to be commanding the mission, so we need to tell him everything that we know."

"Good, then let's sit and I will start the slide of the new evidence."

CHAPTER 21

VALENTINO

Gabe, Rebecca and Cardinal Staff walked out of the conference room and started to head down the hall. Cardinal looked at the two and asked,

"Why did you want to do a sea landing, I don't get it. We did that last time and they will be ready for the attack this time."

"And we will be ready for them. I can a sure you Cardinal, they will not be ready for what is about to happen."

"Why don't you fill me in then?"

"Cardinal, they are not expecting me. I know I can handle them, I almost rather go in alone, or with just Rebecca and I, but Matt insisted that we have the rest of the troops. So, by going in with the boats, but from a different direction, we should be able to take them by surprise."

"You have done this before, so I will take your word on that. What are your plans for lodging?"

"I will find a room at one of the hotels here in Rome."

"Well he can stay at the apartment," Rebecca chimed in, "I have a spare room he can stay in."

"But I thought you said that you live in my old apartment?"

"I did…"

"I didn't have a spare room in that apartment."

"You also didn't have a full kitchen, bathroom, laundry room or a very big living room. Forty years ago, one of the bishops that was doing some of the work here at the Vatican past away and they gave the position to a layperson. So I asked the apartment manager to let me have his apartment and attach the two together."

"So, you remodeled the entire apartment?"

"Almost, your bedroom and part of the living room are still the same. I didn't really touch that part."

"Then I guess that would save some money and if you don't mind me staying there?"

"Well… If you don't mind fighting the bugs for the bed."

Gabe started to chuckle a little bit; Cardinal looked back and forth at the two confused at what was so funny. Gabe looked at Cardinal,

"It's an inside joke Cardinal, I had said something similar back in Nebraska."

"So that is why we didn't get a housing bill from anyone."

"Well, I can make one up for you, if you would like."

"After having to spend that much time with Rebecca, I just might accept it."

"Hey…" Rebecca was feeling the brunt of the jokes now.

"We still love you though, Rebecca." Cardinal gave her a big grin.

Gabe cleared his throat and looked at the Cardinal, "I think that I am hungry and I want to see what my apartment looks like, so let's call this a day and I will get with the troops tomorrow."

"Very well, I will see you two tomorrow then."

With that, the two headed back to the apartment. When they got in the apartment; Rebecca informed him,

"You know Gabe; I don't have much to eat in here. If you want to eat here, we will need to go and get some food at the store."

"No, I have a better idea, let's go to Valentino's and eat there."

"Valentino's, I have never heard of that place. I am not sure that they are still around."

"Oh… I am sure that they are. Let's put away our stuff and we will head down there."

Gabe picked up Rebecca's large bag and his two bags. He took Rebecca's bag into her room, which was his room two hundred years ago. He looked around at the room after he dropped the bag on the bed. Rebecca walked in and asked,

"Is it so different?"

"Surprisingly, it almost has not changed."

"Well… I tried to keep it the same. I liked the way it was, so I kept it."

"I see that, so show me where this new spare room is."

"It is hard to miss, follow me."

They walked out of the room, past the door to the kitchen, through the living room and in the far corner of the living room was a door. Rebecca opened the door and let Gabe peek in. He looked around at the room and smiled,

"You need to update the carpet don't you?"

"If you don't like it, I can let you go to the hotel, where you may be fighting the bugs. There is a convention in town and the only hotels that are available are the cheap ones."

"I'm sorry; it has been a while since I have been invited. I have always been the one providing the hospitality.."

"I understand, but you are right, I have been wanting to pull that carpet up for some time now."

After a half hour the two were standing in front of a door in older Rome. Rebecca looked at the door,

"What are we doing here? There are no restaurants here. This is a residential area."

"That is what we are looking for."

Gabe knocked on the door and a young man answered it. He was about fifteen and stood only five foot two inches tall, He looked up at Gabe,

"Ye… Yes sir? Can I help you?"

"Yes, is your father home?"

"Yes sir?"

"Can you tell him that Gabriel is at the door?"

"Yes sir…"

The young man closed the door and after a few minutes an older man came to the door. He was about five foot eight inches, had brown and gray hair, a scar on his forehead, looked as if he had been working hard all of his life and a big grin on his face. He just stared at Gabe for a moment,

"Gabriel, you are the Gabriel?"

"Yes sir, I am. I hope we are not interrupting anything."

"No, no, of course not, come on in. I'm David Valentino. Did you want something to eat?"

"I was hoping you would ask that. Oh... and this is Rebecca Van Stocks."

"Jimmy…" Dave called out, "Make the table for two. We have special guests."

Dave directed them to the dining room and then went into the kitchen. Rebecca had a strange look on her face and asked,

"How does he know you?"

"Why don't you ask him; I know he will be happy to tell you the story."

Rebecca waited until after they were done eating and were led into the living room. While they were sitting and Mr. Valentino was pouring a bottle of wine for them, Rebecca asked,

"How do you know Gabriel?"

"Where do I start? My family has talked about him for generations." Rebecca looked at him intently as he told the story. "You see when Gabriel was working in Sparta we were, our family that is, his servants. The day that he went to start his mission to fight evil he gave the farm to us."

"You see Rebecca, back in those times; you didn't give your farm to the servants. You sold it to the local people and that included the servants in that. What I did was basically freed them, they were my servants because the family had owed me money and if you were not able to pay it back, you and your family became servants. The people of Sparta didn't like the idea that I gave them the farm,"

"I see, but what are you doing here then?" Rebecca asked,

"Back in 1480 there was a problem with the farm and we had been in contact with Gabriel at that time. So Gabe brought us to Rome to help us out. The agreement was that we would cook for him and other things and he would pay us for the assistance. Even after he left two hundred years ago, he still paid us for any future assistance that we would give him and that includes the meal that we gave you. Now, I have a question for you Rebecca, are you two dating?"

"No, we are not dating."

"That is too bad, we think that he needs to start dating and yes Gabe that was passed down as well."

"I can't believe he would make sure that that was passed down. I gave him my reason on why I don't date."

"Who?" Rebecca asked,

"Tammar Valentino, before I left he kept telling me to start dating. He said that it would loosen me up."

Rebecca gave him a little giggle that they would still bother about that. They spent about two hours there and then headed back to the apartment.

CHAPTER 22

BACK AT THE FANG

Melina was just getting ready to settle down when she heard a knock on her door. She was in just a silk nightgown and didn't want to be disturbed. Jessica was on the other side,

"Melina madam? You have a call and it is very important."

"I'll take it in here then.

"I will forward it then."

After a few more minutes her phone started to ring. She went over and picked it up.

"This is Melina...

The deep male voice came over the phone that she recognized very well. "Melina... We have a problem."

"Yes sir, what is it?"

"I just got word that the last information was incorrect. Gabriel did come back with Rebecca."

"I'm sorry; did you just say that Gabriel did come back with Rebecca?"

"Yes, I did..."

"Ah... That is a problem. Ah... I will have my people pick up the pace, like, right now."

"Good plan... I want a full report in two days."

"Yes, sir... You will have that."

87

She hung up the phone, took a deep breath and then went out in the hall. She went up to Jessica's door and knocked,

"Yes, madam. Is there something I can help you with?"

"What is going on madam?"

"Gabriel is back."

GABE!
THE LADIES
DRESSING
ROOM
IS NOT THE
PLACE TO TALK
ABOUT THE
BATTLE PLANS!

GABRIEL! SIR!
IS THERE SOMETHING I CAN HELP YOU WITH!?

CHAPTER 23

DEPLOYMENT

Early in the morning, Gabe was walking down a long passageway to the back courtyard. As he was getting closer to the yard he could hear the troops talking among themselves. When he walked out into the open; he could see the troops, some were stretching, some were standing in a circle looking at some stuff and others were standing by for something. A tall man was standing among the troops. He was about six foot three inches, silver hair, he had tanned skin, green eyes and looked a very seasoned officer. He looked over to see Gabe standing at the entrance to the courtyard and walked up to him,

"Can I help you, sir?"

"Yes, I am here to help you out."

"Help us out? How are you going to help us?"

"By taking command and I am going to guess General?"

"Ahh... General Michael Cornter. Are you Gabriel?"

"Yes, I am..."

"Oh... Ah... I'm sorry sir; I had no idea who you were. I was expecting."

"Yes I know, that I was a lot taller."

"Well sir, then let me introduce to you the troops under your command."

The troops had already stopped what they were doing to see who the general was talking to. They all have been hearing rumors that Gabriel was back, but none of them knew what he looked like or what to expect, so when they saw the General talking to someone they stopped to see if it was the man of legend. The General walked with Gabe to the troops,

"Gentlemen, can I have you gather around for a moment?" When the troops were done gathering around the General continued, "Gentlemen... I would like to introduce you to Gabriel. He will be leading this mission. Now I know you all have heard the legend of his battles, but I want you to think of him as any other commanding officer that you have worked with. I am sure that......" General Cornter looked at Gabe, "What do we call you anyway?"

"That is a good question. How about for now you can just call me Gabe, if you need a rank though, call me commander."

"I am sure that the commander is here to just finish this mission and then will be going home. I am also sure that he doesn't need too much hero worship while he is with us."

"Thank you, General, for the introduction and I am looking forward to working with you all on this mission."

Gabe then pulled the General aside to talk to him. When he was out of ears reach he asked,

"I don't see Rebecca and she was not in the apartment when I left. Have you seen her yet?"

"She usually goes to the south wing to get ready before we get ready to deploy. I hope you don't mind me talking about your legend? I know the troops are going to be hounding you for information on past battles. I mean, I have to admit that I have some hero worship myself, but this way you will be able to do your job as you so effectively did in the past."

"Ah... Well thank you General, you said that she is in the south wing?"

"Yes sir, it is sort of a tradition for her to go there before the training."

"Well tradition or not, she needs to be here to hear what I have to say and go over everything. I want plenty of time to go over it many times. I will go and get her."

"Very good sir, I will keep the troops busy until you get back."

"Thank you, General..." Gabe felt that something was off, but didn't say anything and started the long walk to the south wing. When Gabe was out of sight one of the captains went up to General Cornter,

"Where is the commander going?"

"He's going to find Rebecca in the south wing."

"But sir, the south wing is the ladies' dressing room."

"Yes... But Gabe doesn't know that. When he left, it was a storage area, it wasn't changed to a ladies' dressing room until thirty years ago."

"Yeah, but shouldn't you had told the commander that?"

"You know... I knew I forgot something."

CHAPTER 24

NEW PLANS

Steve went up to Melina's door and knocked. When Melina answered, she was in her nightgown and was getting ready for bed. She said to him,

"You seem to have a knack of knocking at the wrong times, Steve."

"Sorry madam, but we have guests."

"Guests? What kind of guest could we have that you need to interrupt my time?"

"I don't know, they say that it is important from your contact in Rome." From behind Melina, Jessica asked,

"What is going on?"

"We have guests, I will go and find out what they want. It won't take me long."

Melina walked back in, grabbed a robe and then went back out with Steve. After a few minutes, they were in front of a door with the guests in it. Melina turned to Steve and ordered,

"Go and find out where the Doctor is at. I am sure they will want to know..."

"Very well, madam," Then he walked away.

Melina opened the door when Steve was out of sight and stepped in. Five men were in the room and stood up when Melina walked in. She took a deep breath and said,

"Please have a seat." Four of them sat down and the one that remained standing informed her,

"Melina madam, my name is John, we are here to change the plan just a little bit."

"What do you mean that you are here to change the plan just a little bit?"

"We are going to take the bomb to Rome."

"What? Why? Doesn't he think that my human minions can do the job?"

"He thinks they can, but with Gabriel now involved, he wants to make sure that it is successful. We have an ace up our sleeve."

"And what is that?"

"Me…"

CHAPTER 25

GETTING READY

The halls were as beautiful as Gabe had remembered them. It took a little while to the- to the south wing. There was a door that Gabe didn't remember being there, but a lot had changed and still a lot that had stayed the same. He opened the door and right away he saw a nun walking to the door. He went up to her,

"Excuse me, Sister???"

"Mother Janet."

"Ah... Mother Janet, have you seen Rebecca Van Stocks?"

"Yes, she is down the hall to the right across from the lockers. Second door on the right, but..."

"Thank you, Mother Janet..." Gabe didn't let her finish and took off to the hallway.

When he got to the hallway, he saw the lockers to his left but didn't pay any attention to them. Since it was a storage area when he left; the lockers made sense in storing things in. He found the door that Mother Janet was talking about and opened it, stepped in and there Rebecca sat. All she was wearing was a towel, the room was hot and steam was all over. Rebecca had a look of shock on her face on seeing Gabe in the room and she yelled out,

"Gabe??? What are you doing in here?"

Gabe's face was as red as a stoplight, he turned away and told her, "I was just looking for you, I wanted to go over the battle plans that I have."

"Gabe, the ladies' dressing room is not the place to talk about the battle plans."

"I would have to agree, I will wait for you in the courtyard." Gabe walked out as fast as possible. He was going out so fast that as soon as the door was closed, he ran into another female that was going in. She too was only wearing a towel; she was a young woman, had blond hair and blue eyes and lightly tanned. Gabe had almost knocked the towel off her so she readjusted the towel stepped back and asked,

"Ah... Sir, is there something I can help you with?"

"Ah... No... I don't..."

"Well if you need anything, I am Crystal, just let me know, but not in the ladies' dressing room." She smiled at him and then walked into the sauna.

Gabe left the area as fast as he could. This time he didn't notice the halls as he walked back to the courtyard. In the sauna, Crystal went up to Rebecca,

"Ah... Was that Gabriel?"

"Yes, it was."

"What was he doing in the ladies' dressing room?"

"I think the troops didn't let him know that this is a ladies' dressing room. This was a storage wing when he left two hundred years ago."

"Well, I now know why you are attracted to him."

"What makes you think that I am attracted to him?"

"You cannot pull one over on me, Rebecca."

"He is a colleague and that is it."

"Sure, whatever you say."

"Well... I have to go and talk to Dan and see if he can come with us. I will talk to you later."

"Talk to you later, Rebecca."

Back in the back courtyard, Gabe called over the General so that the other troops could hear what he was saying. The troops looked at Gabe as he called him over and started to chuckle, the General smiled as he walked over. When the General got to Gabe, Gabe started,

"General, I got the hint. I have been gone for some time and I already planned on listening to the ones that have been doing it. That is one thing that was not written in those books about me, I do listen well and you can count on that."

"Good, I just wanted to make sure you understood that sir."

"And by the way, good joke." Gabe smiled at him so that the troops didn't know what he was about to say, "If you ever do that again in front of the troops, I will bump you down so fast you will think that you were a recruit in boot camp again. Do I make myself clear?"

"Very sir…" General was shocked at the sudden comment. From that point, he understood why Gabe was an effective leader. He never let himself look bad in front of the troops. Gabe put his arm around the General,

"Now smile and let's go back to arrange the troops."

"Yes, sir…"

After an hour of setting up the troops, Gabe finally saw Rebecca coming to the courtyard. She was followed by a gentleman that Gabe didn't know, but he wanted to address something else first,

"I am sorry, Rebecca. I didn't know…"

Rebecca held out her hand to stop him and said, "I figured that the troops didn't let you know that it was the ladies' dressing room as a joke, so don't worry about it."

"Thank you, now who is this?" Gabe pointed to the man standing behind her.

"This is Dan; he is the Vatican's nuclear specialist. We brought in a nuclear specialist in about nineteen eighty to help us understand the total threat that was posed by the communist counties and if a nuclear war was started. Dan was working for the United States on all kinds of nuclear devices, and that includes dirty bombs. I thought that it would be a good idea to bring him in on this one."

"Good thinking Rebecca." Gabe went up to Dan, held out his hand, "I'm Gab…"

"Gabriel, yes I know. Rebecca told me all about you on the way here."

"Well, I hope that it was all good."

"You really don't know, do you?"

"Know what?"

"Well, she thinks..."

Rebecca cleared her throat to stop him. He turned to her and smiled. They spent the rest of the day getting ready and going over some of the things that they could.

CHAPTER 26

THE CASE

About midnight Gabe woke up from a bad dream, walked out into the living room and looked at the door to Rebecca's room. He noticed that the door was open and the light was on, He went over to the door to see if Rebecca was awake and found that she wasn't in the room; her gym bag was gone so he figured that she went to the gym close to the Vatican. He got dressed and headed out to the gym. After fifteen minutes of walking down the street and through the Vatican halls, Gabe came to the gym. The room was not very big and was mostly used to keep the Pope and others that work at the Vatican in shape, less health care cost. On one side of the room it had mirrors along with it. Rebecca was off to the right side doing push up. Through the mirror, she saw Gabe standing at the doorway,

"Had a bad dream?"

"How did you know?"

"I heard you when I was leaving; it was about your family."

"You heard all of that?"

"When you have a bad dream, you seem to talk in your sleep."

"Really?"

"Yeah... I heard you one night in Nebraska. I couldn't sleep, I guess I was still on Rome time and I went upstairs for a drink, I could hear you talking. It didn't sound too good then either, other times that I was up and you didn't have any bad dreams you were as quiet as a baby. So

I just concluded that you only talk in your sleep when you have a bad dream."

Gabe took a deep breath and looked down, "I have had too many bad dreams lately and it is not you. They were from before you got there."

Rebecca switched from doing pushups to leg lifts as she asked, "Are they all of your family?"

"A lot of them have been, but they also include old battles or things that have never happened, but I fear that they will."

"You miss your family, don't you?"

"Just like I am sure you miss John."

"Yes, but I was not married to him and didn't have a family with him yet. I could only imagine how bad it was that you lost them all."

Gabe didn't answer; he just looked down at her doing her leg lifts. Rebecca felt that she should have kept her mouth shut on the subject so she said, "I'm sorry; I know that I should have kept my big fat mouth closed." She stood up and walked over to grab her towel.

"No, you are okay. I have come to grips with the past a long time ago."

Rebecca walked up to him; put her hand on his right shoulder. "I know that I cannot replace them, but if you ever need to talk. Well, I am here anytime and you know that I'm not going anywhere. Even if you just do this mission and go home. I want you to know you can still just give me a call."

"Thank you, I just might take you up on that offer," And he gave her a smile, "But I thought I said to everyone to get some rest. What are you doing here at midnight...?"

"I am resting..." She handed the towel to Gabe.

~ ~ ~ ~ ~

Melina was putting some of her stuff in her office when the phone rang. She walked over, looked at who it was from, pick up the phone,

"What do you need Steve?"

"I got good news for you."

"What is the good news?"

"Doctor Kosch is done with the case and wants to do a demonstration."

Melina perked up and informed him, "I will be right down. Go and get the other gentleman and have them meet us at the cage."

"Yes, madam."

Melina put the phone down and walked out of the office. As she walked by Jessica she informed her, "It sounds like the Doctor is done; I am going to see him right now."

"Do you want me to give him a call?"

"No, I want to make sure that he is done first but stand by just in case he is."

"Yes, madam."

Doctor Kosch was working on the case, just under the foam matting. He was installing something under the matting at the base of the case. He was just finishing up as he heard a door open. Quickly he put the matting back in place and waited for them to walk into the glass cage. When everyone was in the cage Melina gestured for him to give his demonstration. Doctor Kosch started out,

"Now, I have not been able to get rid of all the radiation that comes off from the samples that you gave me, but what I have been able to do is hide it." He picked up the sample and placed it in the case. He then closed the case and picked up the detector that they gave him. Then he continued, "As you can see the detector is on and it is not going off. Now I have this switch on the handle, and you can see that there is a light at the bottom of the case." He lifted the case so that everyone could see it, "The light is showing green right now, but when I flick the switch..." The detector went off and the light at the bottom of the case went red. In a loud voice to speak over the detector, "Now the radiation can be detected and the light went red meaning danger of course." He turned the switch back on and the detector went silent. Doctor Kosch finished his demonstration, "Now, like I said, it doesn't get rid of all the radiation, just most of it. So for the person that is going to be transporting it, I wouldn't want to handle it for any longer than a couple of hours."

"Doc, a couple of hours is all we need to transport it." Melina informed him, she then turned to Steve, "Take this down to the others and get it ready. How long do you think that it is going to take now?"

"It should only take a couple more hours now and we can have it off."

"Make sure that the case is booby-trapped as well,"

Melina looked at John, "Just in case you fail."

Steve grabbed the case and left the cage. The others followed him leaving Doctor Kosch in the cage,

"Hey... What about my family? What about letting us go?"

But no one paid any attention to him. He heard the door close and a sad feeling came over him as he looked down.

CHAPTER 27

LANDING IN

The General went up to Gabe and informed him, "We just got permission to use a landing strip on the Southwest edge of Turkey. We were told that it is rocky and it will be hard to find a launching point."

"We will worry about that when we land General…"

The sun was just coming up when two Cl30 Troop carrier planes landed on an open strip in Southern Turkey. They taxied to a large lot for planes that land there. It was not occupied by anyone; for the most part, it was used as an emergency landing or an airport for the local community. On this day, no one was using it and that made it great for the group to set up camp and then get ready to launch the boat. When the first plane stopped, Colonel Wilhelm got out with his troops. They had bags on their backs and some of them were carrying boats over their heads,

"Get in formation!" The men quickly lined up and dropped the boats behind them, then the colonel continued, "Now I want you to set up camp on the far side to the lot in the grass over there." The Colonel pointed to a grassy area and the men darted over after they drop their stuff and started to set up camp.

After the second plane stopped it dropped its back ramp and several more troops ran out with their bags and formed up on the edge of the lot. A Major ran out behind them along with Gabe, Rebecca, and

General Cornter. The Major ordered the men to do the same as the first group and they were off. Gabe turned to Rebecca,

"Can you handle getting the command center set up?"

"Yes..."

"Then you go with the Major and get set up and I will take the General down to the shore and find a good place to launch the boats."

Rebecca smiled at the General as to say, See... He is a good Commander.

The General and Gabe went to the rocky shoreline to find a place to launch the boats, "General, you look to the left and I will look to the right."

"Yes, sir." And the General started to walk along the shore. After about ten or fifteen minutes of looking the General yelled out to Gabe, who was down on the other end of the shore. "I think I have found something!"

Gabe ran over to where the General was standing and looked at where he was pointing. It was a small crop of beach, with rocks on both sides and a path going down from where they were standing. Gabe smiled at the General and complimented,

"Good eye there, General. We will launch from there." Gabe went back up to where Rebecca was setting up the camp. Dan was standing there as well talking to her. When Gabe got close, "The good General found a place to launch the boats. Close to dusk we will launch the boat and the rest of us will board the planes again to drop over the Fang encampment."

"Why didn't you tell that to Matt at the meeting the other day?" Rebecca asked.

"Because I don't like to tell too many people about my plans. It would be too easy for the information to leak out."

"What about me, I am not a fighter. How am I going to get there?" Dan inquired.

"Don't worry about that, your ride should be arriving soon."

"My ride?"

"Yes, I have a different ride for you."

About that time everyone could hear what sounded like helicopters coming in. They looked towards the sea and saw four United States Marine Corps C.H.56 Super Stallion Helicopters and four Cobra Helicopters coming in to land on one of the empty lots. Gabe looked at Dan,

"Speaking of rides, here is yours now."

At that the General came up from the shoreline yelling, *"What in the world is the United States doing here?"*

Gabe held out his hand, "I asked them to be here. Before I left the United States, I made a few phone calls to some friends and told them the problem. The United States Government agreed that if the Fang is successful in destroying the Vatican with a nuclear dirty bomb, it would embolden other terrorist groups to try the same thing and that the Fang will then be unstoppable. Came to find out that there was a carrier that was going to be in the Mediterranean at the same time and the Marines needed some training before going off to Afghanistan. Besides, I never go into a situation like this without back up."

"You told the United States about a Vampire group and they believed you?"

"No… I told them that the group was a terrorist group bent on destroying the Vatican."

"And when were you going to tell us this?"

"When I have the reason to trust you."

"Trust me? I'm the General of these troops and you were wanting to see if you can trust me?!"

"Yes… General, there is something more going on here than what we are seeing, I just can't put my finger on it just yet. I'm trying to find out who I can trust and who I can't."

"What about me, you didn't tell me about this. Don't you trust me?" Rebecca inquired.

"You didn't even tell Rebecca?" The General spat it out as to insult him.

"Actually, that was not on purpose, I forgot to say something to you last night. On that one, I am sorry."

"Is there anything else that you forgot to tell me?"

"The plan that I have. Is the command tent set up?"

"Yes, it is."

About that time the Marine Colonel walked up to them so Gabe,

"Then let me introduce you to Colonel Mattis. Colonel Mattis, this is General Cornter, Brigadier General Van Stocks and Dan the Atom guy." After they were done shaking hands Gabe put his hand on General Cornter's shoulder, "Now that you all know each other, let's go into the command tent and I will go over the plans." Gabe led them all to the command tent.

CHAPTER 28

READY SET GO

Walking into the radar section Melina promptly asked, "What is the problem?"

"There were some helicopters that just flew to Turkey. They came from a United States Carrier in the Mediterranean."

"Did you ask them what they were doing?"

"Yes, they said that it was a training exercise that they are doing with the Turkish Government."

"Well, then I will take them at their word. The United States has done many training exercises with Turkey in the past."

"Very well, madam."

Melina walked out of the station and then went down to talk to Steve. Steve was in the room waiting for the Scientists to get done with the case to send it out. He had been standing there almost all day and was getting tired of waiting,

"How much longer do you think?"

"I don't know. I was told that it won't take too much longer once they had the case ready, but this is getting ridiculous."

Melina didn't waste any time and just went inside the room. It was a glass room, just like the one that Doctor Kosch was in. She quickly asked before they could say something,

"What is taking so long? You said that you could have this done in a couple of hours?"

"Sorry madam, we just had a little problem with the booby trap. The switch on the case where Doctor Kosch put in the dampening device was where we wanted to place the activation switch and we had to find a new place to put it."

"How much longer then?"

"Well, we are almost done actually, about one more hour. We will need to set the timer though. What do you want the timer set for?"

"Set it for noon tomorrow."

"Why noon tomorrow?"

"It is a time that the Vatican will be full of people. Many are going in for the noon Mass and the time that they not going to be expecting us to set it off."

"Yes madam, very good idea."

Melina walked out of the room and asked Steve, "Did you get all of that?"

"Yes madam, I'll go and get the men ready and we will have it out at the location by noon tomorrow."

"I want you to go and make sure that the human minions do their job in protecting John and his men. There is a safe house that you can stay at about ten blocks from the detonation sight. That should be close enough to keep control of them without be in line of the blast site."

"What if Rebecca and Gabriel discover where the bomb is?"

"Well let's hope that John can be a good distraction for them."

"Yes, madam... Is there anything else?"

"No, just go and make sure that the men know that it is almost ready. I have a feeling that the fight is going to be happening tonight, so we want them gone before Gabriel and Rebecca gets here."

"Yes, madam..." From that Steve went to get John and his men ready to go.

Melina walked to her office, it only took five minutes to get there through the tunnels. When she got there she looked at Jessica,

"I want you to take my day copter and head to Frankfurt Germany now."

"Yes madam, but may I ask why?"

"The bomb is almost ready and I have a feeling that Gabriel and Rebecca will be attacking soon. You are not a fighter so I don't want you here for the fight."

"Yes, madam... I will get my stuff and be going in an hour,"

Jessica got up and left for the tunnels to get to her room to pack.

Gabe walked into the tent that Rebecca was using to get herself ready. She was looking over her parachute bag, making sure that it was ready for the drop into the Fang encampment. She looked as if she had done it many times before. He stood at the door just watching her when finally she turned around,

"Is there something I can help you out with, Gabe?"

"I'm sorry, I was just watching you going over your pack."

"You have never jumped out of a plane before, have you?"

"No, but it looks like you have jumped out of a perfectly good plane before."

"I have... I've done sky diving many times before, but I have to admit, this is the first time we have jumped into an encampment."

"Well, this will be my first jump. So I will just watch the pro then."

"Do you want me to go over what I am doing here?"

"If you don't mind?"

"Not at all, come stand beside me and I will show you what to do and what I am doing."

Gabe walked over to her and stood beside her on her left side looking at the bag intently. Rebecca pointed to a metal handle on the right side of the pack, "This is your blue primary shoot. When you jump, count to ten and then pull the handle." Then she pointed to the other one on the other side of the pack, "Now this is your secondary shoot, which is why it is colored red. If the first one fails then pull this one and it should come out."

Gabe reached down and grabbed the red handle to verify, "This is your secondary shoot and that is if the first one doesn't come out," Rebecca nodded to confirm, then Gabe reached around the back of her and grabbed the blue handle, "And this is your primary handle, I count to ten after jumping from the plane and pull this one?"

Rebecca smiled, "Yes, you got it. You should have no problem in the jump." She turned to face him and for a moment they stared at each other. They could feel their faces getting red and their hearts start to race. Gabe then began to step backwards towards the door,

"Well... I ah... Thank you, Rebecca, for that information. Could you umm... Look over mine; I am sure that you will do a good job at it. Umm... I will go and make sure that the boats launch go okay."

Rebecca just watched him walk backward. When Gabe turned around to go out the door, he hit the door frame instead, bounce backward and then turned back around to look at Rebecca, his face redder than before, "I ah..... The door is over here."

Rebecca let out a chuckle as Gabe walked out and then shaking her head, went back to looking over the pack. Outside, General Cornter, Colonel Wilhelm and Colonel Mattis were watching the boats take off, heading for their target. Gabe walked up between General Cornter and Colonel Mattis; the two looked at Gabe and saw that his face was really red. General Cornter spoke up first,

"So what were you doing Commander?"

"I was just having Rebecca go over the packs for our jump. She is checking out our bags to make sure that they are ready for use."

"And you were checking out Rebecca, aye, Commander?" Colonel Mattis commented.

"No... She was showing me the different rip cords on the pack."

"Are you sure you weren't trying to rip on a different cord?" Colonel Wilhelm chimed in.

"How is the launch going, gentlemen?" Trying to change the subject.

"It is going better than we expected, but maybe not as good as your launch with Rebecca." The General stated.

"Do they have plenty of cold water with them?" Still trying to change the subject.

"Yes, they do.... Why? Did you get a little too heated up with Rebecca that you need some water now?" Colonel Mattis asked.

"I think he wanted a little bit of that Brigadier to have a Brigadier Commander." General continued.

"Okay, you three that is enough. Don't you have things that you need to get done?"

"Sure thing sir...." The three smiled at him and then started to walk away. Gabe then spoke up again,

"Colonel Mattis, could you wait for a moment?"

"Yes, sir... What did you need?"

"I need you to keep your helicopter at bay until I call you in. You will be carrying Dan and I don't want him in arms way."

"Yes sir, anything else?"

"Yes... Nothing happened between Rebecca and me, so get that out of your head."

"Sure thing sir, whatever you say sir." He gave him a big smile as he walked away.

C H A P T E R   2 9

THE BATTLE STARTS

The engines of the Cl30's were starting up. Gabe's troops were getting on the plane and finding their seats... Colonel Wilhelm got on the first plane, while General Cornter, Rebecca and Gabe got on the second plane. As Rebecca and Gabe were walking on the ramp, Gabe stopped and looked out at the sunset. It had been three hours since the boats had left and they timed it that it would take that much time to get to the island that the Fang was using. Rebecca looked at Gabe,

"Are you all right Gabe?"

He looked at her smiling face, smiled himself, "Just fine."

"Then let's go... The troops are ready to go and want to take off."

Gabe walked the rest of the way up the ramp and found his seat on the right side of the plane next to Rebecca and across from General Cornter. The two planes started to taxi to the runway. While they were taking off the Marines board their helicopters and they started to take off as well.

In the boats, the men assigned to them had already turned off the engines and were using the oars to get them close enough to the shore that the tide would take them the rest of the way in. The plans were running through their heads. Once the waves were able to take the boats in, or they started to get fired upon, jump out and swim away

114

from the boats, then to shore. In the boat were only two or three men, with ten boats, the number of men totaled about twenty-five. The boats had steel plates made up to look like men in the boats. So to someone on the shore, it would look like about a hundred or so men are coming. One by one the waves started to catch the boats.

On shore, the lookouts for the Fang saw the boats coming in. The commander looked through his spyglass and ordered his men to radio in base camp. "Boats are coming in, what are your orders?"

At base camp, Melina heard the request over the radio and picked up the receiver, "How many?"

Over the radio, she heard, "About ten or so."

"It's Gabriel and Rebecca, open fire. Engage, engage."

Back at the boats all but a few men had jumped into the water and started their swim away from the boats and to the shore when they heard the sound of gunfire and the rounds bouncing off the steel shields in the boats. The last remaining men jumped into the water and began to swim away. It was dark so the ones on shore didn't see the men jump in the water.

Back at base camp, Melina went into her office and grabbed her sword. She knew that they would find their way to the camp. In this way, hopefully they can take down some of their numbers. Outside the sun was down and the guards could hear the gunfire in the distance. None of them were expecting what was coming next.

In the sky, the pilot turned off the engines and started to cost in. He looked back at General Cornter announcing, "We are almost at the drop sight, showing green light."

The General stood up and yelled out, while holding up his thumb to the pilot, "Green light gentlemen, get ready."

On the ground, the men had reached the shore and were getting ready to hit the base the moment that they heard the fighting starting. They took the covers off the weapons and loaded magazines, racked a round into the chamber and sat waiting for the sound of gunfire.

In the planes. the tension was growing waiting for the red light and the signal to jump. They all had gotten their packs on, weapons ready and lined up. Many of them were sweating; Gabe was standing in front of Rebecca. He looked back at her, smiled to ease the tension.

On the shore. the guards were walking down to the boats that were coming ashore shooting them at the same time. When they got to the boat they saw that they were decoys, one of them yelled out, "It's a Trap!!!"

CHAPTER 30

THE FIRST BATTLE

The light went out and the ramp lowered. A gust of wind swept through the plane. As the wind hit each man they felt their stomachs drop. Suddenly the red light lit up the plane's cargo bay and the General yelled out, "Red light, red light, red light!" The General stood in the middle of the bay and the lights went out as the General yelled out to each man as they stepped closer to the door, "Go! Go! Go! Go! Go!"

Each time he hit one of the troops on the pack and they jumped off the ramp and into the blackness of the sky. When it got to Gabe's turn he looked back at Rebecca,

"The last one on the ground buys dinner!"

He ran and jumped out, Rebecca followed yelling, "Hey!!! No fair, you got a head start!"

When the plane was empty, the General then jumped out. They sailed down slowly, looking down; they could see the lights of the camp. They could also see that none of the men were in any rush towards their landing spot. Out of nowhere, one of the men didn't tie down his flashlight good enough and it fell to the ground.

On the ground, one of the guards was walking his post. He had heard the gunfire at the East end of the island only a few minutes ago, but they had just gone silent and he heard on the radio something

about a trap, that they were decoys... Suddenly something fell in front of him only a few feet away. He started to run up to the object.

In the sky above, Rebecca saw the guard running towards where the flashlight fell. She pulled out one of her swords, cut the cords to the parachute and started to drop to the ground.

The guard reached the object that had dropped in front of him; he picked it up and noticed that it was a flashlight. He then looked up and before he could do anything a female figure dropped on top of him and stabbed him in the base of his throat, keeping him from yelling anything.

Rebecca pushed a button on her microphone earpiece, "I'm on the ground and the area is secured."

Back in the sky, Gabe looked at the General, who was floating close to him, "She is good..."

"You have no idea." The General replied.

Gabe and the rest of the troops landed shortly after Rebecca and Gabe signaled to them to spread out and look through the warehouses. With the quietness of the camp, General Cornter went up to Gabe,

"Are you sure that we got here in time?"

Gabe lifted his hand and looked around saying, "No, they are here, somewhere..."

In front of them was a crop of boulders, to their right was the warehouses and a fence went around the camp with guard towers every fifty feet. The boulders in front of them kept the other guard towers from seeing them. They heard over the dead guard's radio,

"It's a hit!"

Gabe's face went pale as he turned around to the troops that were heading to the warehouse and yelled out, "Get down, they know we are here!"

CHAPTER 31

THE HIT

An explosion rocked the camp; the men closest to the explosion were thrown into the air. Five vampires flew out of the warehouse that the explosion came from and landed on the remaining troops. The camp lit up with floodlights, vampires started to come out from all over the camp and attacked the troops. Gabe, Rebecca, General Cornter and the radio man ducked behind the rocks in front of them. Then Gabe looked at the General,

"You were saying?"

"I won't say that again, I promise."

Gabe reached out his hands around each side of his coat and pulled out two pistols, loaded the chamber, stood up and took two shots at the vampires, killing them both. He then ducked down and smiled at Rebecca.

At the far warehouse, Melina came running out. Ten vampires followed behind her, they all had trench coats on and gripped swords in their hands. Melina looked back at them and gave them a nod. They crouched down like lions about to pounce, fangs grew out when they opened their mouths and they leaped into the air, going after the closest soldier to them.

Back at the rocks, Gabe stood up again to take a few more shots at the vampire. He looked at the far warehouse to see the female that had just came out and the vampires jumping into action. Gabe ducked down between Rebecca and General Cornter,

"Well... I now know who the new leader of the Fang is. It's the female that just walked out of that far warehouse wearing the cape of leadership."

Rebecca and the General peeked out from the rock to see this new leader. When Rebecca got a good look she dropped back down,

"That's Melina!"

"Who is Melina?"

"Melina is... Well, that is a story for another time."

"But you do know her?"

"Sadly, yes..."

"Tell me when we are done with this fight."

The General signaled to Gabe that he was moving and to cover him. Gabe stood up and began to fire at the vampires as the General moved to another group of rocks were some of the other troops had taken shelter. Gabe then sat back down and called over the radio men. Rebecca pulled out her two nickel-plated pistols and shot a vampire that was going after the radio men. When the soldier got to Gabe, Gabe ordered,

"Call in the Marines, we need their help!"

"Yes, sir!!!"

Gabe dropped the clips from his pistols and loaded two full ones in, racked the rounds and then smiled at Rebecca,

"You're not going to be able to kill any vampires sitting there."

He jumped over the rocks, killed two more vampires and ran after the ones with the swords. Rebecca smiled and jumped up herself and started to run towards the warehouse were Melina was standing.

Melina saw a man start running out from the rocks that she had not seen before and head to one of the Elite Guard. Then she saw Rebecca jump up from the rocks and head her way. She pulled out her sword and got ready for Rebecca to get to her. Then she signaled the rest of the elite guard to attack the man that came out first.

Gabe saw the other vampires coming his way. He took a few shots at them and quickly noticed that they went faster than the rounds. He holstered the pistols and pulled out his swords. One by one landed around Gabe and lifted their swords at the ready. Gabe smiled at them,

"So... Who wants to die first?"

One of them that had seen Gabe many years ago took a good look at him and recognized him, so he spoke up asking, "Gabriel? Where have you been all this time? I had thought that we scared you off."

"If you did, then why would I be back?"

The one that was directly behind him didn't want to waste any more time and took a swing at Gabe. Gabe twisted around, blocked with one sword and threw the other into his attacker. Instantly the vampire turned to ash. The one that recognized Gabe commented,

"I can see you have not lost your speed."

"In fact, I think I have gotten faster since the last time we fought."

"I will be the judge of that."

He signaled three of them to attack at the same time. Gabe quickly blocked one while cutting off the hand of another and ducking as the third tried to go for his head. He then twisted around again, cut off the leg of the one that went for his head and stabbed the one he blocked killing him.

Up at the far warehouse, Rebecca finally reached Melina and pulled out her swords. She looked at her, "How did you get to be the leader of the Fang Melina?"

"You of all people should know that I have my ways, Rebecca."

"Then you won't mind telling me where the bomb is."

"And that will happen when? Oh... Yah... Never Rebecca. You won't be able to protect the Vatican just like you weren't able to protect me."

"I tried, but when I got there it was too late."

"And it will be too late for you again!"

Melina swung at Rebecca; Rebecca blocked with one sword and then jabbed with the other. Melina jumped back, twisted around, grabbed Rebecca's arm to pull her through the jab and tried to get her from behind. Rebecca swung her sword around to the back of her to block Melina and the fight was in full swing.

It was finally just Gabe and the one that recognized him. The two were going at the fight and Gabe kept dropping him on the ground, but before he could do anything the vampire would block or get out of the way. Gabe looked at him,

"I see you have gotten faster, but are you fast enough?"

"I am fast enough to keep you from getting me."

"Really, are you sure that I am fighting at my full speed. You seem to forget that I'm a little bit faster than vampires."

"Not by what I have seen and besides, your troops are losing this battle."

Gabe looked around and saw all over the troops were getting backed up into a corner. The vampire tried to get Gabe while he was distracted, but Gabe just blocked and threw him to the ground. Then, as the vampire got up, one of the towers was blown apart. He ducked from the blast, looked around to see Marines started to drop from the sky on ropes and cobra helicopters flew overhead firing their rockets at the towers and the warehouses. All at once, the fight turned in the Vatican's favor. Gabe looked at him,

"You were saying?"

At the warehouse, Melina swung at Rebecca, she dropped to her knees, then Melina went down with her sword and Rebecca blocked with her sword by making an X. The Vampire looked at Gabe,

"It's too bad that you couldn't have taught that to Rebecca."

Gabe looked over in the direction of Rebecca and saw the situation. Melina smiled at Rebecca and hissed,

"I have you now."

Rebecca returned the smile, slid Melina's sword to the right and onto the ground, twisted around connecting her left leg against the back of Melina's knees, making her fall backward. She then twisted around again and knocked Melina's sword out of her hand. Rebecca straddled Melina holding one of her swords to Melina's throat and began to yell out,

"Where is the bomb, Melina?"

Again, the vampire tried to take advantage of the distraction and swung at Gabe. Gabe quickly ducked and with his right sword, cut off the hand of the vampire and with his left sword cut off the right leg of the vampire. As the vampire laid on the ground Gabe stood over him,

"Why do people think that position is an end-all position? I knew Rebecca had the upper hand on that one." The vampire's eyes were wide open with the shock of how fast Gabe moved. He tried to slide away from Gabe, but in the end, he knew that Gabe could kill him at any time. Gabe smiled at him, "No… you will not die tonight. Because I have a message for you to deliver…"

CHAPTER 32

THE SEARCH IS ON

Melina was smiling at Rebecca, but not saying a thing. Rebecca continued to yell trying to find out where the bomb is, that is when Gabe walked up to them,

"She won't tell you Rebecca, the bomb is not here."

"How do you know?"

"Because she would not be out here if it was. She would be inside protecting the bomb if it was here."

"Then she knows where it is."

"And she won't tell you."

Five Marines ran up to Gabe to inform him, "Sir, the camp is almost secured, is there anything you want us to do?"

"Yes... Get her up, cuff her and take her away. Call in Colonel Mattis to land here and then get a few Marines to go inside this warehouse and search around for more information."

"Yes, sir…"

Two of them picked up Melina; handcuffed her and took her away. The Marines started to take others into custody; two grabbed some more Marines to help them secure the last of the warehouses. The last called for the colonel to bring in Dan. A helicopter landed on the middle of the camp, Colonel Mattis and Dan jumped out and ran up to where Gabe and Rebecca were standing. Dan spoke up first,

"Where is the bomb?"

"It has left already, we need to find it. I can guess that it is in Rome already." Gabe informed him.

"Then what are we waiting for?"

"I want to see if there is any evidence that might help us out before we leave."

It only took a few minutes, but one of the Marines came out with an older gentleman.

"Sir, I think you should listen to this."

They all looked at the older man as he informed them, "My name is Doctor Kosch, I worked on the bomb. I didn't trust them when they told me that it was just to get some nuclear device off the island. So I placed a tracking device inside the case. The only problem is that, with the radiation of the nuclear material, you have to be within about one to two hundred meters to detect it."

"One or two hundred meters?" Rebecca exclaimed.

"That depends on how much radiation there is in the device and that is not all. I think that they booby-trapped it."

"This is getting better all the time," Dan replied.

Gabe looked at Dan, "Dan... Do you think you can show Rebecca how to disarm the bomb?"

"Without seeing what kind of detonation device that they put in there, it would be hard for me to tell her, why?"

"I rather that Rebecca and I go in alone on this one." Gabe then asked Doctor Kosch, "What is the range on something like that?"

"Depending on the size, given the fact that it is close to the ground or on the ground, it could ring about five to ten blocks radius, but the radiation will go farther than that. I would predict that the radiation could fill half the city if not all of it."

Gabe looked over to see the General walking up and ordered, "General... Call the Vatican and have them evacuate the place and anything around it for about ten blocks radius."

"What about the radiation?" Rebecca asked.

"The first thing is to get people outside the blast area."

"Wouldn't the heat be felt farther than that blast area?"

"The buildings and the ground will contain most of the heat, so the blast and the heat will be contained in the same area. That is not to say that someone close to the area will not get really bad sunburn, plus the blinding light that will follow with the blast."

"Then the only thing to do is to disarm the thing and we cannot fail," Gabe confirmed.

"I will still get the Vatican to clean out the buildings and make sure to clear the area."

"Very good, General." Gabe looked at Colonel Mattis and asked, "We need a lift and can you help out on that one?"

"Yes sir and I'm coming with you."

"Colonel…"

"Commander… I'm Catholic, I will not stand by and let someone destroy the Vatican and besides, you will need some help."

"We may not be successful."

"Your point being?"

At that point, ten more Marines that heard what was going on went up to them and one of them said, "We're going too, we are Catholic and non-Catholic Christian, but we will not let anything happen to the Vatican."

"Very well, I cannot guarantee success, but if you are willing, we will love to have you." Gabe then looked at the General, "Don't you think that you are coming, I will order you to stay. I need you to clean up here and get more information on what we are dealing with."

"Yes sir, I will get right on it."

Colonel Mattis, Gabe, Rebecca and the ten Marines that volunteered for the mission ran down to the helicopter.

ROME HUNT

The family of Doctor Kosch came out as the group bored the helicopter. Gabe could see the Doctor run up to his family and embrace them. The chopper lifted off the ground when everyone was sitting in their seats and started to head west. Through the radio Colonel Mattis informed Gabe,

"Commander!" Yelling over the sound of the helicopter "The Carl Vincent is standing by and ready if we need help."

"Thank you, Colonel."

The sun was coming up when they got close to Rome. Gabe ordered the pilot, "Land in Saint Peter's Square."

"Yes, sir…"

"Colonel, we will go from there."

"What if they see the helicopter, sir?"

"What do you have in mind?"

"If we land at the Pantheon, they won't be expecting us. This way we can sneak up on them. Otherwise, they may just set it off if they see us."

"Good idea… Did you get that, Captain?"

"Yes sir, the Pantheon then, sir?"

"Yes… Land at the Pantheon."

When they landed the Marines, Gabe and Rebecca jumped off and ran away from the helicopter as it took off again. Once the helicopter was gone, the men gathered around Gabe to find out what to do next. Gabe looked at them,

"From here, I believe our best bet is to find a house that is here in Rome. It's about two blocks this way." Gabe pointed southwest towards the Tiber river. They started to run Southwest up the streets to Corso Vittorio Emanuele II. They came to some apartments that were constructed many centuries ago. Gabe began to look around. After a minute or two, Rebecca spoke up,

"If you tell us what you are looking for we may be able to help you find it."

"Yes... I am looking for a door knocker, with the knocker in the shape of a viper hitting a shield."

After about another minute or two, one of the Marines yelled out, "Sir!!! Is this it?"

Gabe ran over to the Marine and saw the knocker, turned to the Marine and smiled,

"Yes it is, very good Devil"

Gabe took a good look at it. The head of the snake was facing to the left and the tail was facing right. He then took a step to the door to the right of the knocker. Rebecca asked,

"What are you doing?"

"Do you see the snake?" Everyone nodded as they looked at it. Gabe then continued, "You see how that tail of the snake is pointing to the right? That indicates that the door we need to use is the right door. If someone knocked on that door, the ones inside will know that it is someone that they don't want. Plus they would often booby trap that door. The door that we need is this one."

Gabe took a step back and kicked the door open. The Marines charged in with their weapons at the ready. When the Colonel, Gabe, and Rebecca went in, the front room was empty. The Colonel looked at Gabe and—asked,

"Are we too late?"

"No, hold on there, Colonel."

Gabe walked up to the left wall that had a bookshelf; he pulled out his swords and then pushed the left corner of the shelf, the bookcase swung open. Gabe put gloves on, jumped in, everyone heard some people struggling and then they saw Gabe come out with a man in a black robe. Gabe threw him down in front of them and everyone pointed their rifles at him. He then walked up to him,

"Where is the bomb, Steve?"

"Do you really think that I will tell you, Gabriel?"

"Yes, knowing you, you have no backbone." Gabe put his sword up to his throat and continued, "If you did, Melina wouldn't be the leader of the Fang right now. Your father was the leader of the Fang before. You should have been the next in line, so that tells me that you have not changed in over two hundred years since we last met in France." Steve just looked at him not saying a word. Gabe smiled at him, "Very well, we don't need you then."

He raised his sword and was about to thrust when Steve spoke up, "Wait!" Gabe drove his sword into his hand cutting it off, the men watched the hand turn to ash.

Gabe knelt down and grabbed his robe, "Yes... Did you have something to say?"

Steve took a deep breath, "They are setting the bomb at Cavall."

"When is it set to go off?" Steve hesitated to say anything, "When Steve, I will not repeat myself."

"Noon...?

"Did you hear that Dan." Dan came in from the outside and lifted his thumb to confirm. Gabe then continued to ask, "Is that enough time?"

"That depends on how long it takes to get there. It is already about ten o'clock and it will take about at least thirty minutes to get there."

"That will give us about an hour and a half to disarm it if Steve is telling us the truth; I guess we should take him with us."

"That would kill me, going out in the sun."

"Your right... But aren't you already dead Steve and since you are no longer of any use to us." Gabe drove his sword into his throat and Steve slowly turned to ash.

"Why did you do that?" Colonel asked.

"He is a vampire, which means he is evil. If we leave him, he will inform the others and we can't take him with us, the sun would kill him anyway."

"Very well, sir..."

It took them about a half-hour to get to the street with all the traffic. The area was quiet, they had cleared out the Vatican already, but Gabe knew that would not stop them from destroying it. They didn't see anyone around for that matter. Colonel looked at his Marines,

"Spread out, keep your eyes open."

"Do you think that he was fibbing?" Rebecca asked.

"No... He was telling the truth for once."

Gabe and Rebecca started to walk to V. D. Crocifisso and when they saw a man down the street with a case in his hand.

Many things happened at the same time at that point.

An explosion at East end of Cavall rocked the area. Gunshots were heard down the west end of the street and the man that they saw; ducked down Crocifisso. The Marines that were not being attacked headed to the points of attack; Colonel Mattis looked at Gabe,

"I will watch Dan, you two go after that man down the street."

And the two took off. When they got to Crocifisso they found the man with the case standing among ten other men. They took a couple of shots at them; Gabe pulled Rebecca behind one of the buildings. He pulled out his pistols and looked at Rebecca,

"Well... I will make a bet that, that is the bomb."

"You think???"

Gabe could still see Dan, he waved him over. When Dan and the Colonel got there he told Dan and the Colonel,

"Colonel, we will draw their fire and get as many of them to follow us down the street. Rebecca, you finish off what is left and protect Dan while he disarms that bomb. Everyone understands all of it?"

"Yes, sir..."They all said at once.   -

Colonel pulled out his pistol and loaded a round into the chamber. Then the two stepped out took two shots each, killing three of them and then took off running down the street, five of them went after the two. When they went past where Dan and Rebecca were standing, Dan pulled out the detector for the signal. It started to beep in the direction of the case, he looked at Rebecca,

"Yep, that is the case with the bomb."

"Good..." Rebecca jumped out from behind the building, took a shot and got the one with the case in the shoulder, making him drop the case and throwing him back. When he hit the ground, he blacked out. The other took a shot at Rebecca; Rebecca rolled to the right out of the way of the shot and got on her knees. She tried to take a shot at him and when he did the same. Rebecca stood up; put her pistols away saying,

"I guess we will have to do this the hard way." She pulled out her swords and so did the other man. They ran after each other and when they met the swords crashed together. The man pushed back on Rebecca and went after her again. Rebecca blocked and went after his legs, she yelled at Dan,

"Go and get the bomb disarmed! I will keep him occupied!"

Dan ran past them and turned off the booby trap while Rebecca continued to engage this man possessed by a demon. Then she heard a very loud voice,

"You got to be kidding me!"

"What is the problem?"

"They set the bomb to the time zone in Turkey."

"And???"

"And we only have a few minutes to disarm this thing."

"You got to be kidding me!" Rebecca replied and then she said under her breath, "Why do these things always have to be so close."

The two continue to fight as Dan quickly; but carefully, disarmed the bomb. The man fighting Rebecca pushed away from her. He was not being successful in stopping her. She was too good and too fast for him, so he said to her,

"So Rebecca, long time no see."

"What??? Have I seen you before?" Demons would often know things that most people didn't, personal things and secrets that people keep inside of themselves. So it came to no surprise that he would know her.

"Look past the demon Rebecca."

"What are you talking about?"

"It's me... Johnny... Surely you have not forgotten the feelings that we shared eighty years ago?"

"But you were killed then, it can't be you."

"Backular brought me back after the funeral and gave me, gave us an opportunity to be together."

Rebecca took a good look and to her shock, she could see Johnny. She took a step back and asked,

"How??? Why???"

"I told you, Backular. This way I was hoping that we could be together."

"But Backular is evil, how could you work for him?"

"Backular cares more than you think. He cared so much, that he came and got me and brought me back."

"Then step aside and let us disarm the bomb, John."

"No..." He barked, "The Vatican is the evil one. They deserve to be destroyed. Look Rebecca, they killed many people in the name of their God in inquisitions all over the world and worst of all they kept you and me apart!" As he talked he kept getting closer to Rebecca. Rebecca looked down; confused at what was going on, but then she remembered all of the times that she saw atrocities and remembered that most of the time a demon or evil being was responsible for them all. She looked up and John was just inches in front of her. What she didn't see was that he had his sword ready to drive into her heart.

"Rebecca... I know you and I can be together forever, just let the Vatican die like it should."

"You don't know me!" She thrust her sword into his heart, he stepped backward in shock and looked at Rebecca, fell to the ground and the demon came out of the body. Rebecca went over and destroyed the demon.

CHAPTER 34

TIME IS RUNNING OUT

When Gabe and the Colonel reached the end of the street, they turned around, took aim again at the pursuing men and fired off two shots. Two more men fell and before the remaining three could fire back, Marines came out of the building and killed the last ones. Gabe looked at the Colonel,

"You got some good Marines there, Colonel."

"You know that no one compares to the United States Marines Corps."

"Let's go see how Rebecca and Dan are doing."

They started to run back down to Crocifisso. It didn't take too long to get back; when they got there they saw Rebecca stab a man in the chest. Only Gabe saw the Demon leave the body, as Rebecca quickly swung at the demon and destroyed it. The others saw Rebecca going after nothing but air. The Colonel looked at Gabe,

"What is she doing?"

"It is hard to explain Colonel, but if you remind me later, I will try my best to do so."

"I will take you up on that then."

Rebecca had a tear fall from her eye; it was as if she had to see Johnny die all over again. Even though she knew that it wasn't him, but the demon that controlled the body. Gabe saw that she was disturbed, but then she looked at Gabe, smiled and remembered something else.

For a moment they forgot about the bomb, then one of the Marines spoke up asking,

"Doc, how is that bomb coming?"

"It will be going better if everyone would keep quiet!"

Rebecca turned around, walked over to stand behind the case. She could see that it only had twenty seconds left; she looked at Dan,

"Ah??? Dan???"

"Shhhhhh!!!!"

Rebecca stood there quietly. Twenty seconds turn to fifteen, then at ten seconds Dan yelled out, "Got it!" But the clock didn't stop the countdown, five seconds, four seconds, three seconds, two seconds, and one second.

C H A P T E R 3 5

DESTINY

The sound made everyone's ears ring, they were all knocked to the ground from the shock wave and smoke filled the air. Gabe quickly shook off the impact of the explosion, stood up and was about to run over to make sure that Rebecca and Dan were okay, when the smoke shifted and he could see the two laying on the ground. Rebecca was on top of Dan...

Moments before

Three seconds, Rebecca grabbed Dan, picked him up and threw him to the ground. She then jumped on top of him to block any kind of blast that came from the bomb. The case erupted in a flash of light and fire, sending parts of the case and rocks into the air. After the smoke started to clear Rebecca looked up. Her right leg was hurting; some of the pieces of the case pierced her leg. She looked down at Dan,

"Are you okay?"

His ears were still ringing and only could see her mouth move, figuring that she was asking him if he was okay he nodded his head. She smiled at him and began to stand up. When Gabe saw Rebecca start to move relief came over him. She limped to where the case was sitting; smoke was all around her, but quickly blowing away. She smiled at him and it made Gabe calm down. As he breathed a sigh of relief, a Marine stood next to him saying,

"She is good at her job."

"That she is..." Gabe responded

Then all at once, three people possessed by demons came out at them from his left and three from his right. He reached across his body with both hands, pulled out his two pistols and started to shoot at them. He looked at Rebecca and the one that she shot in the shoulder came up from behind her and thrust a sword into her back. The blade stuck out from her chest. Gabe let out a yell,

"NO!!!"

At that point, no one could see Gabe move, but to Gabe, everything seemed to move in slow motion. The bullet seemed to take forever to move as he killed the six that were coming at them from the sides. Then he dropped his guns, pulled out his swords. Rebecca started to drop to her knees with the sword still in her chest as Gabe approached. Gabe cut off the head of the man possessed and destroyed the demon before he even had a chance to remove the sword from Rebecca and try to attack Gabe. It all happened so fast that the man was still looking in the direction of Gabe's last location and still had the hideous smile on his face as his head hit the ground. Gabe then grabbed Rebecca as she fell back against him. Gabe laid her head on his lap, Rebecca could barely stay conscious. Dan got up and called for a medivac, the Marines and Colonel Mattis ran to where Rebecca fell. Gabe felt helpless as he heard the sound of sirens coming closer.

CHAPTER 36

GOING HOME

At the hospital, Gabe, Colonel Mattis, Dan, and the other Marines were waiting in the waiting room for some word on Rebecca's condition. Cardinal Staff then walked in and everyone stood up. He went straight up to Gabe.

"Any word yet?"

All Gabe could do was shake his head. Cardinal put his hand on Gabe's shoulder,

"I know that I don't have to tell you this Gabe, but it is all in God's hands now." Then Cardinal gestured for everyone to gather around, "But it doesn't hurt to pray to Him and ask for healing. So let's do some praying now."

They all bowed their heads as Cardinal led them in a prayer. After about an hour the doctor walked out. Gabe and the others turned to face him and hear what he had to say. His face said it all though,

"I am sorry; there is too much damage to her heart. I don't know how much longer she has, all the other wounds have all healed just fine, and if it wasn't for the fact of her ability to heal, she would have been dead before she got here, but the damage to her heart is too extensive. I can't..."

"Can we see her?" Cardinal asked.

"Yes, you can. She is awake and has requested for you and Gabe to see her, but she doesn't know yet."

Gabe went to the room as fast as he was allowed to. Cardinal followed close behind and when Gabe got to the door he stopped at the doorway. Then when Cardinal got there Rebecca looked at them,

"My two favorite guys in the whole world."

Gabe and Cardinal walked in, Gabe stood on her right and Cardinal stood on her left, Gabe grabbed her right hand,

"The doctor says that you are going to be just fine."

"Liar..." She looked at Cardinal, "I am going to tell you that he needs at least an hour in the confessional. You may want to clear your calendar for him."

"Well I will make sure he gets in there then." He smiled at her as he fought the tears from coming out.

Gabe looked at the Cardinal "Cardinal, if you don't mind. I would like to talk to her alone for a moment."

"Not a problem, if Rebecca doesn't mind?"

"I don't mind..."

Cardinal Staff smiled at Gabe and walked out of the room. When Cardinal was gone Gabe looked at Rebecca, as she asked,

"Okay, what do you want to tell me?"

"I want you to close your eyes, don't worry, I will be right here the whole time."

She gave him a strange look so Gabe continued, "Trust me, rest your eyes, I will be here holding your hand the whole time."

So Rebecca closed her eyes and as soon as Gabe could tell that she was asleep he began to pray.

CHAPTER 37

THE SQUARE

After a few minutes, Gabe came out of the room. He went up to Cardinal Staff and told him in a somber tone,

"It is done…"

Cardinal put his hand on Gabe's left shoulder, looked into the room and saw Rebecca with her eyes closed and not moving. He let out a sigh,

"She is with God now, a better place than we can imagine."

The nurse walked in after hearing what Gabe was telling the Cardinal, Only moments after she walked in she ran out yelling,

"Doctor!!! Doctor!!! Come quick!"

The doctor ran into the room and started to run out to get his scope and as he started to run back in, Cardinal stopped him,

"What is going on?!"

"It's a miracle!!! It is simply a miracle!!!"

"What?!"

"Her heart has sealed itself. I don't know how, but she is going to come out of this after all."

Gabe smiled at the Cardinal, "You know, I think I better let the Marines know that she is going to make it after all."

All Cardinal could do is look at Gabe with his mouth wide open as he walked away to the waiting room.

A week later, Gabe was walking through Saint Peter's Square when Rebecca saw him and ran up to him. She had just gotten out of the hospital and wanted to see Gabe right away. As she ran up to him she yelled out,

"Gabe, wait!"

Gabe stopped for a moment to let her catch up. Once she was beside him he started to walk again.

"So, how are you feeling?" He asked her.

"Better than ever before. I hear I have you to thank for that one. Cardinal told me all about what happened. I didn't know you had the gift of healing?"

"I don't…"

Rebecca had a confused look on her face but quickly shook it off. "Well, I hear that the Day Hunters have taken over the camp on the island of Crete. You know the one that the Fang had. I think we should have a plan together and be ready to go in about two weeks."

"Well, you handle that one Rebecca. I waited for you to get out of the hospital, but now I need to get back to Nebraska."

Rebecca's heart dropped, stopped in the middle of the square, she looked down and let out a sigh, "I guess we did agree to that and you stayed longer than the agreement." She couldn't look at him as she finished, "I hope your farm is successful and maybe someday we might meet if I get a mission in the States." At that, she stormed off trying to hold back the tears from falling.

Gabe yelled out to her, "But Rebecca…" But she didn't listen and kept going.

A couple of weeks later Rebecca was boarding the Vatican 747 heading to Greece to start her next mission. They were planning on kicking the Day Hunter werewolf group out of Crete. She had wanted to drive there, but Cardinal insisted on her taking the plane. She walked past the command center and when she got to the conference room she could hear some of the men talking. Suddenly she saw a figure lean over and say,

"Late again... I think I need to get you a new watch."

Rebecca almost fell over, she walked up to the seat in front of her, "I thought that you were going home, what happened?"

"You didn't let me finish. I needed to go back to Nebraska to pick up some more clothes. I didn't have enough to continue to fight evil. So have a seat and let's get a-going."

She smiled and sat next to him. As the plane lifted off the ground, Gabe started to tell Rebecca about the first time he came to fight the werewolves.

EPILOGUE

A man was standing on a balcony overlooking a nighttime mountains scene. He was a tall man, about six foot three inches, had white hair with dark roots, His skin was tanned and had the look of age, though most people would put him at fifty to fifty-five, he was much older than that. His suit was tailored to him, but it still looked like if he flexed, he would still tare the thing at the seams. He had his right hand over his left shoulder, rubbing a scare that he received many centuries ago. His thoughts were interrupted when his assistant came to the door to announce,

"Backular sir... Melina is here to see you."

He didn't look back at her, just told her, "Very good Karen, send her in."

"Yes, sir..."

Karen stepped to the side and waved Melina through. When Melina crossed the threshold of the door to the balcony, she stopped before continuing on, bowed and announced herself.

"Backular sir..."

"How did you get away from those Marines?"

She stood straight and smiled, "I have my ways. Gabriel made the mistake of leaving me with them."

"No Melina, Gabe never makes mistakes; he wanted you to get away."

Melina looked down and took a deep breath. She knew the next thing she had to do. "Backular sir, I am sorry that I failed you."

"No Melina, you didn't fail me. In fact, you did more than I expected."

A confused look came to her face as she replied, "I don't understand, I didn't destroy the Vatican like we planned. Now Gabriel is back working for them and Rebecca is staying to help him out. With the two, I don't know if we can hold out."

"Melina, Melina... You found Gabe's weakness; you showed me how to destroy him once and for all. Destroying the Vatican was just the extra bonus. I wanted Gabe back and that was about all for now, but you found his weakness and that was more than I expected."

"Sir???"

"I have a new plan for you Melina. Gabe and Rebecca are going to Crete to remove the Day Hunters from there. I want you there as well. I have a special mission for you."

"Yes, sir?"

"That I will tell you later, for now, go and get the special room set up."

"Yes, sir..." As Melina bowed and turned around she remembered something and looked back at Backular, "Oh... I almost forgot... One of my elite guardsmen had a message for me from Gabriel and he wanted me to pass it along."

"What is it?"

"You're next..."